lying, baking, & surfing

THERESA HALVORSEN

NBBP

Copyright © 2024 by Theresa Halvorsen

All rights reserved.

No part of this book may be reproduced in any form or by any electronic or mechanical means, including information storage and retrieval systems, without written permission from the authors, except for the use of brief quotations in a book review.

The story, all names, characters and incidents portrayed in this production are fictitious. No identification with actual persons (living or deceased), places, buildings, and products is intended or should be inferred.

ISBN: 978-1-955431-19-4

For information about special discounts available for bulk purchases contact www.nobadbookspress.com

To Brad, for all the support, love, and for moving us to San Diego

one

"SO, you're saying you're completely out."

Sabrina looked helplessly at the older gentleman in front of her. She'd already told him the bakery was out of the hot cross buns he'd come in to purchase. She'd apologized and had even looked through the racks of baked goods in the back just in case there was a tray of the goodies she'd missed.

There wasn't. And she knew it. She'd burned them all this morning. It was only her third day at Sugar Bliss, and she'd managed to set the oven at 450 degrees rather than 350. It wouldn't have been a big deal, but hot cross buns required multiple rises. The damn buns had taken her two days.

And she'd burned them all.

"So there's not another rack in the back that you missed?" The gentleman was in his sixties, just starting to stoop and thin out. He chewed on his gray mustache while he stared into the glass case displaying Sugar Bliss's goodies—the breads, and the unique rolls like teacakes, sticky buns, and crumpets—like he could force the hot cross buns to materialize if he just wished hard enough.

Sabrina pushed down her frustration and humiliation. "I do

apologize," she said yet again. "But when I popped into the back, I talked to Hattie, the owner. She's sorry, but we sold out of those hot cross buns early and won't be able to make any more for the rest of the week. The currants and candied orange peels are back-ordered—supply chain issues," she said with a shrug, hoping her red cheeks weren't giving her lie away. "But we should have them for next week. I can set some aside for you when I make them again."

"Hattie's hot cross buns are my daughter's favorite," the man groused, chewing on his upper lip. "I promised her if she'd stay at my house rather than a hotel, I'd get her the hot cross buns as a thank you."

Sabrina felt terrible. She'd taken on this job to knead dough. To smell flour, yeast, and sugar as they mixed and baked. To create tangible things that people enjoyed. To—as her yoga instructor taught—enter a meditative state when baking (ok, when doing anything) and forget about the rest of the world.

Forget about the last few weeks if nothing else. She hadn't taken this job to ruin someone's day by setting the oven at the wrong temperature.

"I'm sure she'll understand," Sabrina said. She used her shoulder to nudge a strand of her curly hair out of her eyes. "These things happen," she continued. "Everyone is struggling with supply chain issues now."

The man rubbed his head, like he wasn't sure how to move on without the buns. Like his entire day was set around picking up the buns and then the rest of his to-do list would fall into place.

"Is there another type of pastry she would like?" Sabrina finally asked when the silence got to her. "Our cinnamon rolls are fresh this morning, and we've got some new sticky buns with a butterscotch drizzle. If your daughter likes hot cross buns, she may like those."

The man sighed into his steel-gray mustache and Sabrina felt her face shift into the leadership mask, the blank face all corporate leaders achieve when annoyed and hiding it.

She'd just be quiet and wait for him to tell her how to help him. Silence could be an effective tool and one she used frequently with the other C-level executives she worked with.

Used to work with, she corrected herself.

The man's phone buzzed, and he looked down, triggering a memory. *Wait a minute,* Sabrina thought. She knew him. It was Mathew Dicing. He used to be the HR director at Thinkfling, where Sabrina had spent the last fifteen years. *Oh god, did he remember her?*

"I'll give you a twenty percent discount on the sticky buns," she said in desperation, wanting him out before he recognized her and asked why on earth she was working in a bakery rather than at Thinkfling. "I haven't met a customer yet that hasn't liked them." It was true, though she'd only been working in the bakery for a few days, but he didn't need to know that. "And I'll have Cloey, the afternoon cashier, call you as soon as I make more hot cross buns. Hopefully, early next week."

"My daughter's coming in tomorrow."

"We won't have them by tomorrow," Sabrina said, wondering if maybe she could go to another bakery, buy some hot cross buns, and try to sell them . . . hell . . . give them to her former coworker before he recognized her. "I'm sorry," she said hating how repetitious and useless that phrase was.

Sabrina remembered this man when his mustache was dark brown, before he'd started to stoop from the weight of time. She remembered going to him with a problem employee and following his advice to protect the company and be an empathic, though respected, leader. She remembered how HR had seemed to flounder without Mathew, without his guidance.

He'd left an enormous gap both in knowledge and capability Thinkfling had never fully recovered from.

Had she left a similar gap or was her former job doing better without her? Thomas, the CEO, had certainly thought things would be better when he'd told her it was best if she'd resigned.

Immediately. She hadn't even been allowed to say goodbye to her teams.

She pushed the thoughts away, pushed away those memories of that meeting, pushed away how terrible the last two weeks had been. Her new life working in this bakery was to mix ingredients, knead dough, and occasionally work the front counter. That had to be enough for right now.

"Did you want the sticky buns or not?" she finally asked Mathew.

"How about a sample, Matt?" Hattie said, coming out from the back room where she kept her office and the ancient computer she used to store her recipes and attempt inventory control. The owner pulled the tray out from the glass case and chose a bun, placing it onto the counter and cutting a small triangle from it. She passed him a sample and popped another into her mouth. "I'm very proud of this recipe. I think you'll agree it's one of my best. And I made this batch myself."

Sabrina tried not to bristle at her tone. Hattie had been obviously angry with Sabrina this morning as they'd thrown the blackened hot cross buns into the dumpster outside and aired out the kitchen of the burnt orange and dough smell.

Mathew chewed and swallowed the bite of dough, his eyes lighting up with bliss for a second. That was Hattie's secret. Somehow the baker managed to infuse a bit of joy with each of her creations. Sabrina was lucky to learn from her.

Truly, she reminded herself.

"I'll take a half-dozen of the sticky buns," Mathew finally decided. "And I appreciate the twenty percent discount."

Hattie twitched but said nothing about the discount, merely wishing the customer well and heading back into her office without speaking to Sabrina. Sabrina packed the rolls into a white box and tied it with a bit of blue ribbon, the only signature thing Hattie did. The bakery didn't even stamp the boxes with their name, Sugar Bliss, and bought the plain white boxes in bulk off Amazon.

"I'm sure your daughter will enjoy these," Sabrina told Mathew as she rang him up.

"I hope so," he said. "I'm hoping she'll come visit more if I've got her favorites in my house."

Sabrina's eyes wandered to his hand as he counted out the change. No wedding ring. Hadn't he been married? She vaguely remembered congratulating him over the birth of a grandbaby right after she started at Thinkfling. Maybe his marriage hadn't been able to survive Mathew's retirement or hadn't survived the pressure from Thinkfling. Her own marriage certainly hadn't survived her career and its demands.

After Mathew left, Sabrina spent a few minutes tidying up the counters, wiping off bits off sugar and drizzle, and then sweeping up the crumbs. Sugar Bliss in Encinitas, north of San Diego, was a local favorite. It hadn't been updated since the eighties if the scuffed walls with shabby mint-green paint and faded framed pictures of milkshakes, teacakes, and crumpets were anything to go off of. Luckily, Hattie's baking gift had kept the place in business, rather than the decor.

Sabrina's phone buzzed, and she whipped it out of her pocket to find a text notifying her of a sale for a brand of work pants she no longer needed. She'd been so used to responding immediately to requests for her help and now, oddly enough, there were no emails, texts, or Teams messages demanding her time. Just ads and random notifications.

Sabrina sighed and tucked her phone away. For years, she'd

been telling whoever would listen that she wanted a vacation, wanted out of the 24/7 world of her previous job, that she was burnt out and aching for an opportunity to try something else. As her yoga teacher had told her, she'd put that desire out into the universe so many times, the universe had responded.

And she'd gotten fired. And now kneaded dough.

Hattie came out, her graying hair held back by a purple headband haloing around her face.

"Twenty percent off?" she asked Sabrina. "Why the discount? He has plenty of money. More since his wife died."

Guess that explained what happened to the wife.

"I was trying to make a sale," Sabrina said, resisting the urge to put her hands on her hips. "Figured a sale was better than no sale. And he was frustrated we ran out of his favorite buns."

"Matt and his family have been through a lot the last few months. He's trying to help his daughter but can't figure out how. So he buys her sweets, hoping it'll help." Hattie tugged on her lip for a second. "Just offer him a sample of whatever sweet bun we have next time, and he'll buy it without the twenty percent discount. We can't afford to lose any more money."

"Well, when you get the candied peels and currants in, you should announce it on your social media," Sabrina said. "Tell everyone you made a new batch of hot cross buns in the morning. Bet you'd get a ton of sales that way."

Hattie's frown deepened.

"You know what I mean," Sabrina continued. "Those 'Now Available for a Limited Time!' posts on Facebook or Instagram. I see those all the time on my feeds from various bakeries."

"I don't have time for any social media," Hattie said.

"Oh!" Sabrina said. "You should. You can pay someone. Actually, Cloey could probably do that for you. Her generation is so good at that stuff and since she's not a professional, it wouldn't cost that much."

"No one cares about social media," Hattie said with a sniff. "Just a waste of time." She went back into her office and slammed the door behind her.

What had she done wrong? Sabrina turned, her elbow hitting the stack of white boxes and knocking them to the floor. With a sigh, she bent to pick them up just as the front door opened with a jangle of the bell attached to the knob. Turning back toward the door to greet the customer, Sabrina shifted, her foot landing on a box, which slid out from under her.

Down she went.

two

"OH MY GOD," Cloey said, running behind the bakery counter and helping Sabrina to her feet. "You ok?"

Sabrina rubbed her hip where it had landed against the floor. "I think so." Her cheeks flushed red.

"What happened?" Cloey asked.

"I knocked over the flattened boxes, stepped on one, and then slipped," Sabrina muttered. She felt okay overall, though her knees were shaking. Adrenaline and embarrassment probably.

"You gotta be careful," Cloey said, bending over to help her pick up the boxes then sliding them back onto their place on the counter.

"I know. I'm betting Hattie doesn't have workers' comp."

Cloey's face dimpled. "I'm betting she doesn't." She looked Sabrina up and down. "You sure you're ok?" she asked again. "You look pretty shaken."

Cloey was the college student Hattie had hired to work at the counter in the afternoons since she and Sabrina had to be up so early to make all the goodies. Cloey primarily sold the morning's baked goods to high school students and tourists, then bundled up any leftovers and took them to Father Joe's—the local homeless shelter.

"I'm hanging in there," Sabrina said, untying the flour-dusted blue apron Hattie had assigned her from around her waist. "But I think I made Hattie mad," she said, surprising herself. At her corporate job making people mad hadn't really bothered her. It was part of executive leadership. But now she questioned everything and everyone. Had she said the right thing? Were her actions correct? Getting fired from Thinkfling had cost her more than a job; she'd lost a part of herself, of her identity.

It's just a phase, she reminded herself. A normal part of the grieving process. A normal part of trying new things.

"Hattie gets mad easily now," Cloey said. "Don't take it personally." Nothing seemed to bother Cloey and Sabrina enjoyed her co-worker's ease and fluidity with life. "It's her problem, not yours," the other woman continued. "Don't let her get to you."

"You're right," Sabrina said, trying to regain her equilibrium. She dumped her apron into the dirty linen container and grabbed her water bottle. "Hattie is Hattie, and I'm not responsible for her emotions. It is outside of my control."

Cloey raised an eyebrow. "Are you reading that book from that yoga instructor I recommended? The one on letting things go and not trying to control everything?"

"I read most of it last night. I mean there's a few key takeaways." She ignored Cloey's snort of humor. "I like the idea of identifying the things you can't control and then letting them go. I think I got too used to being prepared for everything and anything and trying to anticipate what might go wrong, and—"

"Now you stress about things going wrong that haven't gone wrong yet?" Cloey leaned her hip against the counter.

"Exactly. And those things might not even happen, but if

they do, I'm prepared." But she hadn't been prepared for losing her job. It had never occurred to her as a possible outcome.

"If you're still looking for something to read, that yoga instructor has a great book on mindfulness too. And yoga and the meditation practice will help you learn to be more mindful."

Sabrina resisted rolling her eyes. Meditation was the hardest part for her. "I've been trying," she said. "It is peaceful, but my brain doesn't stop chattering very well."

Cloey went into the back, grabbing a tray of teacakes and refilling the glass case. "The point of meditation isn't to get your brain to stop chattering. It's to notice the chattering and the accompanying emotions. Because your brain doesn't ever stop. Even the best meditators in the world don't get their brains to stop chattering. They just observe it and let it go."

"Oh." *Then what was the point?*

"Remind me of how long you've been doing yoga again?" she asked.

"Two weeks."

Cloey smiled, her teeth a flash of white against her dark skin. "Give it time. You've been through a lot, and I would imagine your emotions are still pretty strong. You may feel like you're going crazy, but you're just going through the normal process. I like your new look, by the way."

Sabrina had gone shopping in some of the bohemian shops in the touristy part of town, buying thin gauzy skirts and tunic tops to wear at the bakery, instead of mismatched and uncoordinated leggings and old button-up blouses. She'd always liked the bohemian look—though had never been brave enough to try it—and today had paired a purple patterned skirt with some dark leggings and a black tank top. She'd even added rows of cheap stones and beads around her neck.

"It's not too much?" she asked Cloey, noticing Cloey's casual t-shirt and jeans that looked amazing and effortless. "Or am I too old for this look? Or not laid-back enough? It's just I've realized I don't have many non-work clothes."

"It suits you," Cloey said, straightening from bending over the case and looking her over. "You're not ever going to be a 100% free-spirit and shouldn't try. You're just exploring other facets of your personality. And changing your outfit is a great way to explore. If you don't like it, wear something different. It's not like you're getting tattoos or shaving your head."

"I'm trying," Sabrina said, her heart suddenly pounding with anxiety. It felt like everything had happened to her so quickly.

"Now's the time to try something different," Cloey said. "Time to explore who you might become, if you take a different path. You're more than your job."

"This might be the hardest thing I've ever done." The words seem to float through the air between them. An admittance Sabrina had no clue what she was doing.

Cloey pursed her lips. "Sometimes I feel like if we're becoming stagnant, the universe will force a change."

"The universe is an asshole," Sabrina said.

"It is," Cloey said with a laugh. "I'll see you tomorrow."

three

SABRINA SAT in the parking lot of Sugar Bliss watching a couple holding hands walk past the bakery without glancing in the window and duck into the funky gift shop next to the bakery. Watching them made her heart ache, but for what she didn't know. She wasn't interested in starting a relationship, didn't need any more stuff for her house, and didn't really enjoy shopping.

Maybe it was having something to do that was lacking. Right now, she had no plans, no place to go, nothing to do. Working for Hattie was much better than sitting around trying to binge-watch all the Netflix shows she'd promised herself she would watch if only she had the time. Now she had the time, but just didn't want to. It seemed like such a waste to spend her life sitting on a couch.

Her afternoon and evening stretched out in front of her—a whole lot of nothing. Her house was clean, the laundry, and grocery shopping done. Her to-do checklist of things like bills, watering plants, and scheduling a visit with her GYN was complete. Maybe she could swing by the grocery store, pick up some ingredients for a new recipe she could pick at random off

Instagram. Maybe a gooey, cheesy something she'd eat with sliced baguettes.

Sabrina shook her head. After spending all day mixing ingredients and kneading dough, the idea of cooking didn't sound fun. She could order in, yet again, she supposed, but was tiring of the delivery options close to her house. Besides, that would only solve the question of dinner. What did others do in the evenings without work reports to review, proposals to write and delegate to others? What did they do without the corporate trappings of A3s, SWOTs and monthly analysis? She was sick of not finding interesting shows to stream, sick of taking baths with novels she'd seen advertised on Facebook. She missed the after-work drinks, the cocktail parties, and various executive events she'd pretended to hate. She missed getting dressed up for an evening out and continuing the game of office politics.

Sabrina closed her eyes and took a deep yoga breath. She needed to focus on what she could control. She couldn't control that she was in a different phase of her life. She could control what she did with her time. So why on earth was she going home to mope around her empty house? Tourists came from everywhere to San Diego; she should get out and do some exploring, see those touristy places she'd never gone to.

She put her Tesla into drive and drove toward Moonlight Beach, flipping on a podcast as she went. It was early afternoon —plenty of time before sunset to walk across the sand, get some fish tacos from a food truck, and enjoy the sunset at one of the picnic benches. All the stuff she'd said she would do if she had the time.

Well, now she had it. So, she was going to enjoy it.

God-fucking-damnit.

The traffic wasn't cooperating though, and Sabrina tapped her fingers on the steering wheel, waiting for a light that was only letting two cars through at a time. Maybe she was being silly, heading to the beach in the middle of the day. The light turned green, but the driver at the front of the line wasn't paying attention and only went after the light turned yellow. Horns blared. *Sitting here certainly wasn't soothing,* Sabrina thought. A burst of laughter from the podcast she was half-listening to caught her attention.

"You don't seriously do that?" the male voice asked.

"I do," the female voice said. "If I'm going to be stuck on a plane or a bus or even at a boring work event where no one knows me, I'll pretend to be someone else."

"Like you walk around pretending to be that other person? Or are you introducing yourself as that person? And how do you pretend to be someone else?"

"So here's how it went." The woman stopped to giggle. "On this plane when we were stuck on the tarmac, I imagined I was a mom with two kids and a cheating husband that I left at home, and I was going to my high school reunion where I wanted to hook up with my old boyfriend. And I came up with the name Bianca."

"Bianca?"

"I stuck with my first initial, B, and that's surprisingly limited."

The traffic inched forward, three cars making it through the light, though the last one ran it. Horns blared again and Sabrina sighed.

"So what did Bianca do?" the male voice asked. "I mean like how did you start the conversation?"

"That was the best part," the female podcaster said. "I just leaned over and asked the other person if they were traveling for vacation or work. And they said, 'vacation.' And I said, 'me too.' And then I pretended to hedge and then be like, 'well actually it's mostly pleasure, but also some business. I mean I plan to network. It's my high school reunion.'" The female podcaster's voice had changed, getting higher pitched and breathy.

"Oh my god," the other podcaster said. "I would've put in my earbuds and refused to make eye contact with you."

"Right?" the woman giggled. "But when you're stuck on the tarmac, people are bored, so if they think there's some tea, some gossip, they'll listen to you. This couple seemed super interested in what I was saying, so I just kept going. I told them all about my made-up kids, my no-good husband, and that I was super excited to reconnect with old friends, if you know what I mean."

"That actually sounds like my high school reunion," the male podcaster said.

"Yep," the woman said. "That's the key to pretending to be someone else. It has to be believable."

Sabrina was through the light! She turned left and the turquoise ocean—the sun glinting off the waves—came into view. A few more blocks and she pulled into the parking lot at Moonlight Beach where families were loading up coolers, beach chairs, and sun-drunk children, buckling them into their SUVs.

"The best part is how freeing it is," the female podcaster continued. "I'm never going to see these people again, so I literally can become who I want to be. I don't have my past, or my job, or my relationships interfering with who I want to be in that moment. I can be anyone. I've been a fiction writer, a nun, a butcher, a kindergarten teacher, an actor no one knows who starred in a bunch of commercials no one remembers. I can be ANYONE. It's really freeing."

Sabrina betted it was. Who would she be if she could be anyone? Because right now being a fired executive and a terrible baker who was probably also going to get fired, kind of sucked.

Nothing came to mind.

four

WITH A FRUSTRATED SIGH, Sabrina climbed out of her car, threading her way past tourists and cars battling for parking spots. One child wailed as he was buckled into a car seat and the tired parent promised ice cream back at the hotel if they would just stop. Judging from the gigantic sigh from the mom as she closed the car door, he wasn't going to stop crying anytime soon.

Sabrina climbed the steps down to the beach, stopping to help a parent trying to carry a net of toys, a bag of wet towels, and an ice chest. She walked the woman back up to her car. After being thanked with an alcoholic seltzer water that Sabrina refused, she went back down the stairs for the second time.

The afternoon sun baked the sand, and children and adults played in the surf. Giant rocks pounded into place by the sea provided hiding places for crabs, giant anemones, and other oceany things. Teenagers, splashed by the surf spray, climbed across the rocky terrain, exclaiming as they peered into the cracks and crevices. Most tourists had some sort of easy-up or umbrella shading their patch of sand from the sun. Two men, their shirts off, muscles rippling, threw a football back and forth to the admiring glances of many women and some of the men.

They were probably Marines from Camp Pendleton, Sabrina thought.

For a second, she wondered what it would be like to be one of those women who could go up to a handsome man like that, giggle, and flirt. Eventually share a kiss, then a ride to an apartment or a hotel for a night of casual sex, never to see each other again. Could she pretend to be that person? A flirter, fully comfortable in her sexuality, comfortable in the idea of casual sex, of just being with someone for a night and nothing more? What would that person's career be? What would they do with their free time? Hike? Go to the wineries in Temecula? Travel?

Sabrina had it! This person would be a successful pottery person (a potter?) with her own gallery of sculptures that were sold all over the world. She would travel and have casual sex in all sorts of interesting, exotic locations.

The football landed at her feet and one of the Marine guys waved at her to throw it back. She picked up the ball and started to walk it over. She could do this. She would introduce herself as a pottery person (a potter, damnit!) who traveled all over—first class—she added mentally. And this person has lots of casual sex because it helps with the pottery muse.

She handed the ball to the closest guy, all tanned and muscular, like out of a movie.

"Thanks," he said barely glancing at her before throwing the ball to the other Marine.

"I'm—" Damn. What would her name be? Should she give her name or another? God, this was a stupid idea.

"Look," the guy said before she could say anything. "I'm married, he's married. We're not interested. Just came out to throw the ball back and forth."

Sabrina felt her cheeks flush and embarrassed sweat coated her hands. "Of course," she said. "Have fun."

Fine. She didn't want to talk to him anyways. She walked away, following the surf.

After a minute, she chuckled. Even if she had figured out how to pretend to be a potter, she barely remembered how to date. It had been so easy back in college when she and Leroy met at a party, went out to dinner a few times, made out in his car before going back to her place for what she now knew was some awkward sex. But from there, it had been easy to move in together and then get married.

Their divorce had even been straight-forward too, with a few quick signatures, the sale of their house, and moving into their new and separate places.

But the idea of dating petrified her. She didn't even know how to go up to a guy she didn't know, even pretending to be someone else. What would she talk about? How would the night evolve? Would it end with her going back to his place? Or hers? There were the questions like what kind of underwear was she wearing and when was the last time she'd shaved her legs? Or would her conversations be so boring he wouldn't even want to go back to his place with her?

Her stomach danced with nerves. This was too much pressure. Okay, dating was off the table for a while. And she shouldn't be pretending to be someone else. She didn't even know who she was right now. She needed to focus on healing, and what she wanted to do with her life anyway. Yoga, meditation, and listening to the universe was her focus. Not dating.

Sabrina kept walking south and eventually kicked off her Converse, stuffing the socks into the toes and lacing them together. The sand was painfully hot, so she headed closer to the water to walk in the damp sand, shading her eyes against the sun's glare. She dodged lost sand toys, giant holes, the remnants of sandcastles, and bits of seaweed and sharp rocks. Every so often, a shell would catch her eye and she'd bend over to collect it into the toe of her shoe. Using the strategies she'd been learning in yoga, she tried to be in the moment, in the present and only worry about what she could control. She focused on the coolness of the water over her toes and the soft sand. She stopped to note the blue water crested with white foam moving sand, shells, and tiny rocks back and forth.

In the distance, surfers waited in the water for the perfect wave. She stopped to watch them, marveling at their athleticism, their balance, their focus. The sun moved across the sky; the water rippling back and forth over her ankles, the sand eventually enclosing her toes and then her feet. It was almost like it was telling her to stay right here.

A seagull swooped overhead, and she startled. God, how long had she been standing there zoning out? Multiple seagulls flew over her head, landing on a brightly colored towel where a bag and an ice chest waited for their owner. The seagulls' sharp orange beaks pecked at something on the towel. Sabrina shaded her eyes against the glare of the sun. Was that a sweatshirt the birds were picking at? The owner must have left food in a pocket. More seagulls swooped down and tugged at the cloth.

Pulling her feet from the sand, she yelled and began to run toward the towel, waving her arms. The seagulls squawked and two of them grabbed the sweatshirt and picked it up, beginning to fly away with it. With a scream of rage, of pent-up anger for the last two weeks, she ran faster; the sand kicking up in her wake. With a "mine-mine" of anger, the seagulls dropped the sweatshirt and a bag of chips fell from a pocket. The seagulls swooped at her, not wanting to let their prize go.

Picking up the bag, she flung it as far away as she could. The seagulls followed, ripping apart the packaging and fighting over the salty potatoes with cackles and squawks. Laughing and cradling the sweatshirt, she headed back toward the towel. She probably shouldn't have bothered; it was a gray hoodie, ripped in the shoulder with a faded Padres emblem. The rip looked new, probably caused by the seagulls. Folding up the sweatshirt, she wished she'd brought a piece of paper to write a note to the owner explaining the situation.

Though she didn't know what she would write. *Seagulls tried to kidnap your sweatshirt, but I saved the day! Though you did lose your chips.*

Ridiculous.

Turning back toward her car, the sun bright in her eyes, her toe connected with a rock half-buried in the sand. Flailing, she dropped to her knees while white hot pain radiated up her foot. Sabrina blinked away tears.

Son of a bitch, that hurt.

She inspected her toe, half expecting from the level of pain, to see it lying a few inches away from her body. But it looked like it normally did, though a bit red.

"Holy god," a male voice said. "Let me help you up."

His blonde hair was damp from the waves, his dark body suit partially unzipped, showing tanned muscle. "I can't believe you ran after those seagulls!"

"Oh," she said, realizing she'd probably put on a show for the surfers. "I just saw them attack the sweatshirt and wasn't thinking."

He helped her to her feet, his hands gentle on her elbow. "You ok?" he asked. "Did that rock get you?"

"I'm fine." She fought her windblown hair out of her eyes, wishing she'd remembered a sunhat or at least a headband. She must look terrible, her hair tangled, and her skin reddened from the sun and wind.

"Well here, that's my sweatshirt you saved, so thank you,"

he said. "I totally forgot about the chips in the pocket. And I know better. Those stupid seagulls go after everything."

"They do," she said with a laugh.

"Yeah, I'm sorry. But thank you." He was handsome, with his blonde hair, blue-green eyes, and a multiple-day beard, darker than the hair on his head.

God, she wished she could flirt. He was so handsome, a perfect distraction for her thoughts. "One of those things," she said becoming perky. "Happy to help though. One of those things. You know seagulls." She tried giggling, but it just sounded deranged. "I'll . . . see you around." She mentally winced. *God, what an idiot she was.*

"I'm Jonathan," he said. "Johnny. Do you . . . do you want to get a cup of coffee? As a thank you, of course. The waves are dying, and I'm getting tired of paddling back out."

He wanted to buy her a coffee? She'd just been thinking about how hard it was to start a conversation with a handsome guy and not only was the conversation started, but he was asking her out. But he was also surfing in the middle of the day, which meant he probably didn't have a job.

But did that matter? It was just coffee. He was super handsome. Maybe she could try some flirting, work on that skill. If he was terrible, if she was terrible, she could finish her drink and leave within fifteen minutes if she wanted.

And it wasn't like there was anything waiting for her at home other than an evening of takeout and flipping around Netflix trying to find something to watch.

"I'm Breena," she said. "I teach yoga."

five

BREENA HAD AGREED to the coffee—Jonathan hadn't thought she would. She was definitely out of his league, beautiful and laid-back, wearing a bright purple skirt that clung to her legs. She'd even paired it with Converse instead of flip-flops, creating this vibe of someone who didn't care what others thought. Not only was it different from the appearance-conscious women who lived in the San Diego suburb of Encinitas, but he could tell she'd be completely different from his last girlfriend, who'd been so regimented about what she did, thinking through every option, terrified she'd make the wrong choice.

Out of habit, he'd almost offered Breena four different coffee shops within walking distance and had to stop from pulling up reviews on Yelp so she could choose the "best" place.

But he'd paused at the last minute, choosing the coffee shop he'd had breakfast at that morning. It wasn't a Starbucks, but it wasn't anything super touristy either; just a quiet place with comfortable chairs and tables where he'd spent his morning grading papers.

Breena had helped guide his surfboard into his jeep as

they'd stored his belongings. He'd appreciated how she'd volunteered to assist him without being asked and the way she kept tugging her curly hair from her eyes.

"So, you're a yoga instructor?" Jonathan asked as they started the walk to the coffee shop and stopped at a crosswalk for the light to change.

She blinked, started to answer, then with a small smile, said, "Yep. I have my own studio and everything."

"That must be interesting," he said, tucking his hands into his pockets. That explained why she'd been at the beach in the middle of the day—her studio was probably the busiest in the mornings and evenings. "Though I don't know anything about yoga."

There was a flicker of . . . some emotion across her face. Was it relief? That was odd. Maybe different types of yoga were controversial or something. Or it was something yoga instructors argued about. He didn't know. "I've always wanted to get into it though," he said.

"It's definitely . . . fulfilling," she said. "Though the business part is so much work. More than you'd realize. It's so hard to keep a business open in expensive San Diego. What about you?"

"Surf instructor," he said. "Own my own shop and everything. And I totally know what you mean about keeping a business open in San Diego. It's a lot of work." The lie slipped out so easily, without any thought, like how he'd shortened his name. When he'd been driving to Moonlight Beach he'd been listening to his favorite podcast—Weird Rants—and Brandy, one of the hosts, had been talking about how she'd pretend to be someone else on long flights. He'd liked the idea but hadn't been planning to implement it without thinking it through.

Well, it was too late now.

"We should do a trade," he said. "You'll show me how to do yoga, and I'll show you how to surf."

"Agreed," she said with a tight smile. "But I do have a favor to ask."

Oh great. She hated the coffee shop he'd offered. Maybe he'd offended her with the offer of coffee. Maybe she preferred some free-range drink place that sold mushroom water instead of coffee, guaranteed to give you the same energy boost, but that tasted like slimy mushrooms.

But as the light changed, and they started crossing the street, she said, "I love yoga, but that's my career, and I don't want to bore you with Chak . . . ras and Oms and Asanas and I could go on and on." She laughed and tucked her hair behind an ear. "And I was thinking, can we just talk about interesting stuff? Like movies or books or . . . like . . ." she faltered. "Interesting things, for lack of a better term. I'll even take politics, science, or religion, or even practicing mindfulness. But just . . . who cares what we do to make money? Aren't we more than that?"

Jonathan fought to not let out a puff of relief. He could talk about surfing, but he didn't know anything about running a business. What did someone who owned a surf shop do? Sell surf boards? Rent body boards to tourists? Did he have staff? He'd always heard business owners complain about making payroll—he knew nothing about that and probably couldn't lie well about it.

"Agreed," he said. "I'm a movie buff, so that'll keep us busy for a while." He opened the door to the coffee shop for her, the smell of roasting coffee surrounding them. "I can talk all you want about movies."

"Oh wow," Breena said, looking around, her eyes wide. "This place is awesome."

The owners of the coffee shop had gone for a library or study vibe, placing deep leather armchairs, leather couches, and dark wood tables with a fifties feel. There were interesting things like typewriters, record players and even an ancient movie projector scattered around on tables and shelves. "I didn't know this place was even here," she said.

"It's a hidden gem. Are you from San Diego?"

She smiled as they stepped up to the counter to order. "Hot . . . tea," she said with a blink to the purple-haired woman working the counter. The woman offered her a list and Breena analyzed it before choosing an herbal one. "I live around here. Been in the area for about fifteen years. I used to spend all my time—" she paused with a head shake like she'd changed her mind about what she was going to say. "I didn't know this place was here. Now I do, and I'll be back."

Jonathan placed his order, and they took a seat on a large couch. She pulled the throw pillow from behind her back and cradled it on her lap, turning her body and folding her legs up so she faced him. "So, what's your favorite movie?" she asked. "Or is it like a TV show or a book where it depends on your mood or what you're looking for?"

"Exactly," he responded. "But I'm a sucker for zombie movies."

"Zombie?" She thanked the server delivering her tea and nestled the mug between her fingers. "That's not what I thought you'd say. I thought you'd start with something intellectual, like a documentary or something you'd watch in a film class."

He laughed. "Actually, the zombie genre is surprisingly diverse."

six

OVER THEIR SECOND cup of coffee (tea for her), they talked about mindfulness and why Shaun of the Dead was better than World War Z. It was more nuanced, Jonathan explained, though the book *World War Z* was well-written and worth a read. He then excused himself and stepped away from Breena and onto the sidewalk outside to make a phone call.

"Hey Luz," he said to his school's admin assistant. "It's Jonathan. I'm not going to make it back after all. My doctor's appointment is lasting longer than I thought it would."

He could feel her disapproval over the phone and resisted hunching his shoulders, like a high schooler getting scolded. He thought back to something Breena had said about the universe. She'd shared how the universe flows through humans, and that unhappiness comes from trying to control what you can't. While he'd normally have discounted the woo-woo-ness of that, today it made sense. It reminded him of surfing and that moment when the waves flowed beneath and around him, his body in balance with the board, the air, and the movement of the water. That moment when everything was perfect and nothing else existed, other than him and the wave. Everything else was outside his control.

He couldn't control Luz's dislike of him. Lily's death hadn't been his fault. What had happened was outside of his control. He'd done everything he could to help that teenager. Besides, it shouldn't be Luz's business, anyway. She'd barely known the girl. Barely knew any of the students at their school. She was admin and only cared about schedules and paperwork and making sure everyone followed the rules.

"You know how doctors' appointments are," he mumbled. "By the time I get out of here and make it back to school, I'll be there for fifteen minutes. Just tell my sub to keep going with the lesson plans I laid out."

"You laid out the whole day?" she asked, her voice a whip.

"Well, you know how doctors are." God, he was repeating himself now. He'd actually been planning to go back to teach his afternoon classes after spending the morning surfing. But in case he'd injured himself or hadn't felt up to it, he'd planned out the whole day. And fuck her for judging him. He could take a mental health day if he wanted to. He had the sick time saved up and almost never used it. And he needed to take a day sometimes. Everyone did.

But Johnny, surf instructor and surf shop owner wouldn't have any awareness of this. Cool surfer Johnny wouldn't care what Luz thought of him.

"Bye Luz," he said. "I'll review any emails or parent needs once I'm home. Dude, I even hope you have the great day you're obviously having."

He snickered as he hung up, pleased Johnny had managed to work the word "dude" into the conversation. But Jonathan—the teacher—winced a bit. He shouldn't have been quite so mean to the school's admin assistant. It was a hard job to manage all the students, parents, and teachers' needs.

He stuffed the phone back into his pocket and glanced through the window at Breena. She was staring at her phone, frowning at something on the screen. With a small shake of her head, she closed whatever app she was on and stuffed her phone back into the large patchwork bag she carried.

During their conversations, she'd never once pulled out her phone, not even to check the time, and he'd appreciated how she didn't just leave her phone on the table next to her while talking to him. "Nothing was more important than this moment," she'd said at one point when they'd both heard her phone buzz and she'd refused to check it. Though when it had buzzed again, she'd winced and said, "Least, I'm trying to be more in the moment."

Maybe she could teach him how to be more flexible and fluid with things. His ex-girlfriend certainly hadn't. And Breena was interesting to talk with, especially with the no talking about work stuff rule. He hadn't realized how much work had driven conversations with others. This had been one of the better dates he'd ever been on, and he wasn't ready for it to end.

His eyes landed on an old movie theatre, the ancient La Paloma Theatre, the marque sign bright in the sunlight. Sometimes they showed marathons during the week. He glanced back through the window at Breena. She was watching him, frowning slightly. He gave her a one-minute gesture, and she smiled and nodded, going back to her tea.

A quick search on his phone told him the old theatre was doing a daytime movie marathon of Evil Dead. They were such classic, campy horror movies, especially Army of Darkness. She'd probably hate it. She was probably a pacifist, socially liberal, and spent her free time volunteering with the homeless or animal shelters. He could see her working with animals.

But what if she loved it? What if watching a horror comedy

was her perfect way of spending an afternoon, like it was for him?

He went running back into the coffee shop. "Want to go see a movie?"

"Now?"

"Now!"

"I... what... um..." She closed her eyes for a second. "I'd love to," she said. "And I don't even care what movie it is."

So, they watched Evil Dead 2 and Army of Darkness back-to-back, each of them snacking on popcorn dripping with butter, though she'd refused a sugary soda. Between movies he'd jumped up and gotten a package of junior mints and sour patch kids which she'd looked at longingly before refusing with a "sugar's really not good for meditation."

During Army of Darkness, she chuckled at just the right moments, understanding the campy humor. But he loved watching her during the jumpy moments, when she'd pull her hoodie up over her face, peek out, wince, and then go back into hiding.

His heart was lighter than it'd been in weeks.

"Do you have anywhere to go after this?" Breena asked when they came out in the early evening, a sunset painting the sky in purples and oranges. "Like home to a family, or hanging out with friends or anything?"

"I have nothing," Jonathan said. That was a lie. He had a mountain of grading to do, but he didn't want this day to end. "My... assistant is running the shop right now. We'll be closing soon, and he can handle that."

She thought for a second. "I have nothing either. I will tell you that I don't have a family or other obligations at home. No husband or boyfriend. I don't even have a cat. I used to have a fish, a beta someone gave me, but it died. I don't think I took good care of its water."

That interested him; she'd seemed like the type who would have a cat, at least, if not a whole zoo of critters. But the no boyfriend thing was the best part.

"I don't have a family either," he said. "No girlfriend. I have a dog. A giant lab named Lando."

"Lando?"

"Lando Calrissian."

He saw the blank look on her face, then she tilted her head to the side and said, "Star Wars, right? From the original ones made in the '80s?"

"Right."

"I've seen some of those. My—I knew someone super into that. That and Harry Potter. Maybe I should watch Star Wars. Have a marathon; something to do." Her eyes looked sad for a minute, and he wanted to make her smile again.

"There's actually a marathon next weekend down in La Jolla," he said. "The first three movies and by first three, I mean the originals with Luke, Han, and Leia. Would you want to go?"

"Maybe," she said with a smile, the sadness gone from her blue eyes. She glanced over her shoulder at the parking lot their cars were in. The sun was sinking into the ocean, the marine layer creeping closer to shore. "Do you . . . want to get some dinner? Popcorn only fills me up so much. There's plenty of places around here."

He had work he needed to do, grading primarily. He was behind on getting his freshmen their essay back on how Lincoln changed history with his choice to have Andrew Jackson as his vice president. It was his favorite essay to read; he loved how the thirteen and fourteen-year-olds tugged apart history and then drew conclusions about the United States' current political process.

But Jonathan couldn't get enough of this woman, her smiles, and the way her curly hair kept blowing into her face.

He couldn't wait until she'd let him brush it out of her eyes, tug it behind her ears. He loved how relaxed she was, able to just drop everything on a weekday to hang out with a total stranger to watch zombie movies. Most of the women he'd met thought through choices like that, balancing work, and family needs. And then often said they were too busy. Or just didn't like the things he did.

"I'd love to have dinner," he said. "What do you like?"

"I'm not picky," she said. "Though I'm starving."

"Then we'll walk and see if anything jumps out," Jonathan said. "There's lots of restaurants in the next few blocks." He thought about taking her hand, but that seemed too presumptuous. A thought occurred to him. "Ok, I have to ask," he said. "Are you vegetarian or vegan? I know that can make it hard to eat out even in San Diego. My sister tries to be vegetarian but says it's really challenging and there's lots of meat and butter hidden in stuff."

"Oh, that's a good point," Breena said with a tight smile as she straightened her beaded bracelets. "I guess we'll have to check the menu, though I can find something at most restaurants. Salad, hold the chicken—that type of thing."

"Great," Jonathan said. He was glad she wasn't vegan. He didn't have a problem with people choosing a vegan lifestyle; it was just hard to find places that had 100% vegan food. And he liked going out to eat and trying new restaurants when he dated. And to him, fish tacos were practically a food group.

After a few minutes, they passed a chalkboard sign that proclaimed Italian food was available down a narrow street, barely big enough for a car, and closed off at the end. No wonder the restaurant needed the sign.

"Let's go this way," he said, grabbing her hand.

"Wait, where?"

seven

JOHNNY DRAGGED Sabrina down the narrow street, his hand warm around hers. It was always odd how these old buildings put businesses down side streets where no one could see them. Sabrina supposed the rent was cheap, but she knew from her previous job, the amount of marketing they'd have to do ate into any savings.

"Let's try this place," Johnny said, opening the door into what looked like an Italian restaurant. "Pasta is vegetarian, right?"

"Right," she said. The truth was—she liked burgers and steaks. And bacon and pulled pork sandwiches. And fish tacos. Those were practically a food group to her and the best part of living in San Diego. But not eating meat for one night couldn't be that hard.

There wasn't anyone waiting in the lobby or around the hostess desk, which was always a bad sign to her. But there were a few tables with couples and the yummy smell of garlic, oregano, and tomatoes.

Her stomach rumbled, and she hoped Johnny hadn't heard it.

"Let me just—" She dug around in her giant hobo bag for her phone. Her fingers closed around the case, but she let it go. Yoga-loving Breena wouldn't check Yelp reviews. Breena would just go with it, like with the surprisingly fun movies she'd watched that afternoon. Besides, what was the worst that could happen? Bad food that she didn't like? She could always not eat it.

Though paying for a meal you didn't eat and didn't like sucked. And food poisoning would suck worse if she was being honest. Sabrina mentally shrugged. Too late now.

The hostess appeared and showed them to a table in the middle of the restaurant. She passed out large, laminated menus, Sabrina's with a sauce stain on the corner. Sabrina tried not to wince. Whelp, if she got food poisoning, she'd get a story out of it at least. That she wouldn't be able to tell anyone about because all her friends still worked at Thinkfling and would wonder why she hadn't checked the reviews before sitting down.

Maybe this pretending to be a free-spirited yoga instructor wasn't such a good idea. But Johnny was interesting, and she was going to try to enjoy herself, even if she had no idea why she'd told Johnny she was a yoga instructor named Breena, of all things.

She read through the menu, peeking up at Johnny when she thought he wouldn't catch her. He tugged on his lip as he scanned the menu, his hair still mussed from the ocean water. God, he was so good looking, her mind tended to scatter when she looked at him. And he seemed to like her. At least she thought so. He wouldn't have agreed to go out to dinner with her if he didn't, right?

She needed wine. She flipped the menu over to peruse the wine selection before wincing. Would Breena drink wine or would she be a clean-eating, no alcohol, kind of yoga instructor? Nope—Sabrina decided. That was going too far. She couldn't be expected to give up meat AND wine.

A server, wearing the cliché white shirt and black apron tied at his waist, brought them a breadbasket, and a small plate with oil, vinegar, and herbs. Johnny offered the basket to Sabrina, and she refused with a shake of her head. She'd been eating more carbs than normal since taking the job at the bakery, and she'd likely end up with pasta tonight anyway. With a shrug, Johnny removed the cloth covering. Yeasty focaccia, thinly cut and smelling of flour and herbs, wafted upward. She watched him dip the bread in the oil and take a bite. His eyes closed.

"Oh my god," he said. "I've never had bread like this in my whole life. And I've eaten at some fancy places."

He passed her the basket again. Telling herself to go with the flow and not worry about the calories, she took a small piece and dipped it into the oil. She took a bite, the bread melting on her tongue, the herbs in the oil a perfect accompaniment to the herbs in the bread.

"Oh my god," she said, her mouth full. "If the bread is this good, how is everything else?"

"Can I start you off with something to drink, maybe some wine?" the server asked.

"I'd love a glass of your house red," Johnny said.

House red. Sabrina tried not to sneer. House reds were often a terrible blend, cheaply made and designed to make everyone happy with no imagination or definition to the wine. But would Breena know or care?

"I'll take the house red as well," she said. "Is it a blend?"

"It's a Tempranillo."

Sabrina raised an eyebrow.

"The owner has his own vineyard in Spain and enjoys

unique varietals of grapes. He likes to surprise his customers," the server said with a small smile.

"He really does," Sabrina said, forgetting who she was pretending to be. "I think I've only had a Tempranillo without it being added to a wine blend a few times. Sounds perfect."

The server nodded and went to place their order at the bar.

"So, you know wine?" Johnny said. "I gotta admit, I didn't see that one coming. Plants, animals, dreams, chakras, all that stuff, I would've assumed from a yoga instructor. But not wine."

Son-of-a-bitch.

She felt her boardroom face shift into position; her give-nothing-away-face. This pretending to be someone else was hard. "I've just picked it up a bit here and there," she said. Could she point over his shoulder and say, "What in the world is that?" and get away with it?

Probably not.

"I'm sorry," Johnny said. "Is wine one of those things we shouldn't talk about? Did you date a sommelier and it ended badly?"

Sabrina breathed out. She'd brought up the wine and commented on the Tempranillo. And it wasn't Johnny's fault his question reminded her of the early years with her ex-husband Leroy. How they'd go wine tasting and host wine parties on Sunday afternoons with their friends; the bottles kept in their wine fridge and pulled out only for special occasions. Those were the years before she'd been promoted at Thinkfling and had to work on the weekends or was too tired to go anywhere.

"I'm sorry," she said. "I do know about wines, but it's been a while since I did more than just have a glass here and there. And no, I didn't date a sommelier." Inspiration struck. "I used to work at a winery in college." She could see Breena doing that. In fact, Breena likely had several different jobs, all of them interesting and things she learned a lot from. Breena would be about the journey, not the destination like Sabrina was.

"Interesting," Johnny said. "I know nothing, but I think growing the grapes for wine is nuanced right? The weather has to be exactly perfect, or the grapes will taste different."

"Exactly," she said. She took a sip of her wine and expanded on her lie. "This little town outside of Sacramento had all these wineries, and I'd get to pour wine and educate people all about it—they didn't listen well, because they'd been drinking and were often pretending they enjoyed the wine, but they had fun." She'd been to enough wineries to be able to make that part up at least.

"Did you go to Sac State or UC Davis? My mom lives in Sacramento; Davis is a fun little town."

Seriously? She'd picked Sacramento because she knew it did have wineries in the hills but didn't actually know anyone who lived there. If he asked her questions about Sacramento, she was in trouble.

"I went to Davis," she said and only because she'd attended UC San Diego and figured they couldn't be that different. "Go . . ." dang it, what was their mascot—she just remembered it had a weird name. Luckily, the server delivered their wine before she could make a fool of herself and get caught in her lies. He poured her a sample; she swirled and took a sip. Cherries, fig, and a hint of tobacco burst in her mouth. She swallowed. "Holy god. That's incredible."

"We do sell it in bottles," the server said.

"I will probably take some home," she said.

He grinned and offered to give them a few more minutes to look over the menu.

Sabrina read the menu again and decided to forgo the spaghetti and meatballs—her favorite, damnit— for a Caesar salad with the heavy dressing on the side—no wait! Shit!

Caesar dressing had anchovies and those were fish that Breena wouldn't eat. Fighting back a sigh of frustration she decided to just have the boring house salad with a balsamic vinaigrette. But she was going to eat the croutons if she couldn't have meat!

"So, what are you going to get?" she asked Johnny, hoping the server had distracted him from asking her about UC Davis and Sacramento.

"Meatballs and spaghetti, I think." Sabrina resisted an eye roll. Of course he would. "Normally I'd get a salad, but if the bread was that good . . . I don't know. I've had such a great time; I don't want to ruin the night with a salad."

Whelp, she didn't want to ruin it with a salad either. But she was also having a great time. Having a salad so she didn't get caught in her small lies was a small sacrifice.

"Well, I'm going to get a salad and finish off the bread," she said swiping the last piece.

The server glided back over to take their order. Within minutes, a small side salad came out for Johnny with a fresh basket of bread Sabrina claimed as her own.

"I wonder why this place is so empty," she said. One other couple had come in and, judging from the yummy noises coming from the other end of the restaurant, they were having the same experience she and Johnny were. Or having sex.

"It's a Wednesday?" Johnny said with a shrug. He had a flick of creamy Italian dressing on his chin, and Sabrina leaned forward and ran her finger over it. He held his eyes with hers and she felt her cheeks turn crimson. She wiped the dribble on the napkin on her lap.

What was wrong with her? She was pretending to be a yoga instructor and had chased down a seagull, met a stranger, then had coffee, a movie, and dinner; all completely unplanned. Since her divorce she'd gone out on a total of two dates, both forced on her by friends. She'd met both men at the restaurant where they had reservations and then spent the evening chatting about jobs or college or something equally boring that showed how intellectual they were. Neither of them would've taken her to see a campy horror movie like Army of Darkness.

That was probably why her previous dates had ended in the restaurant parking lots with them promising to text each other, but never doing it other than a "thank you" text a few days later. She'd chalked it up to being out of practice with dating and not really wanting a relationship, anyway. Work was—had been—more important.

She was kind of liking this Breena who wasn't focused on work and could go see a movie in the middle of the day. Besides, with Johnny, everything felt natural. There was something to be said for that. Maybe she'd been chasing the wrong things. She was divorced, fired from her job, and while she had a nice house, a nice car, and enough money for vacations—at least, for the moment—maybe the tradeoff hadn't been worth it.

Their meals came and Sabrina tried not to drool as she watched Johnny cut into a meatball and bring a bite trailing spaghetti into his mouth. She did have to admit after a bite of salad, that the lettuce was super fresh, and the creamy Italian dressing was amazing.

"So, tell me why you like campy horror movies so much," she said, cutting a tomato into a bite sized piece.

They each had a second glass of wine, and shared a slice of cheesecake, all amazingly balanced and perfect. Johnny paid—no drama, no pretending that they'd split it—he just took the check and together they walked out, him holding the door open for her and then curling his fingers around hers. His hand was warm and soft. She caught him glancing at her to gauge her reaction, seeing if she would pull away. She squeezed his hand slightly and smiled up at him. He smiled back and then their arms collided with a pole.

It didn't even hurt; Sabrina was enjoying herself so much. Laughing, they dropped their hands and then rejoined once past the pole.

They were quiet during the walk back to the beach parking lot. She didn't want the night to end, but she wasn't ready to go back to his place. Not yet. That was a touch too laid-back even for Breena.

"Oh no," Johnny said with a groan. The gates to the parking lot were closed and padlocked. He pointed at the big sign telling them the lot closed at sundown, and it was way past sundown.

"Shit," he whispered, running his hands through his hair. "I can't believe I didn't suggest we move the cars after the movie. I didn't even think about it. And I know this lot closes at sundown."

Maybe it was the wine or the carbs from the bread, but this disaster wasn't fazing her. Her house wasn't that far away, and she could take an Uber home and then back to her car in the morning. Heck, she could take an Uber to her job and then an Uber to her car if she wanted to sleep in for an extra fifteen minutes.

"Not a big deal," she said. "Thank goodness for ride-sharing apps."

Johnny smiled, his shoulders dropping. "You're right. This isn't that big of a deal. He stepped closer. "Do you want to . . . share one? I mean, if we're going in the same direction, of course."

eight

JONATHAN STARED into Breena's blue eyes. Normally he'd have been pacing around, trying to figure out how he could get his car out of the parking lot, annoyed he'd ruined tomorrow morning's routine, annoyed he'd have to get up early to get back to his car, annoyed he'd have to leave his surfboard and hope no one stole it.

But all he saw were her eyes. A strand of her hair blew into her face, and he reached over to tuck the lock behind her ear, like he'd been imagining. She smiled, just a bit, and he moved his hand to her chin, cupping her face and touching his lips to hers. He went in gentle, but she gave a soft sigh, relaxing into him. He increased the intensity, slipping his tongue between her lips. She tasted of wine and garlic.

And peace.

His heart rate increased, pumping warmed blood to his extremities, but his soul quieted, the worries of the last few months fading away. There was just this moment, just the feel of her lips on his. Her hands reached around, gripping his waist, pulling him closer to her.

Breathless, she broke the kiss, but rested her forehead against his, catching her breath.

"So, about that Uber," he asked, silencing the voice in his head asking him what on earth he was doing.

In answer, she kissed him again, deeper and more intensely, her lips almost bruising his. She nipped at his lower lip while her hands found the bare skin between his shirt and pants. He gasped at the cool touch, a perfect counterpoint to his heated skin. Jonathan moved his hands down to cup her butt and ran his lips down to nibble on her neck. She let out a soft moan, and he contemplated asking if they should just find a hotel. Come back to their cars in the morning after a walk of shame. After the perfect way to end their perfect day.

"God, I want to bring you back to my place," she whispered into his ear, her lips sending tremors down his legs. "But not tonight. We just met."

Breena stared into his eyes, and he kissed her again, gentle, and sweet. A promise of more when she was ready. But she moved her head, and his lips traveled down her neck again. She nibbled on his ear. He lost control, lost his plans to be gentle, to take things slow. He slid the strap of her top off her shoulder, kissing her collarbone and tracing his thumb along the side of her breast.

Finally, she moved away from him with a joy-filled laugh. "Ok, I'm getting a car, just for me. And no, I won't share it." But she picked up his hand and kissed the knuckles to take away any sting.

Jonathan pulled out his own phone, ordering his own car. When he looked back, she stared at the ocean, the half-moon reflecting on the smooth water. She made a slight movement, wiping her cheek on her shoulder.

"What's wrong?"

"Nothing," she said, glancing at him and then back at the

water. "I think the emotion of the day just caught up with me. It's so beautiful and today was a perfect and amazing day." She wrapped her arms around his waist and stared up at him. "Whatever happens next, thank you for that. This was truly one of the best days I can remember for a while."

He kissed her again, not on the lips, but on the tears running down her cheeks.

"I promise you," she said with a laugh, wiping them away. "They're not tears of sadness. And I'm not some creepy crazy person who normally cries after being kissed, either."

He laughed, enjoying her. "I know you're not." They turned toward the ocean, and she rested her head on his shoulder, and he wrapped his arm around her waist. They watched the waves move back and forth, the silvery moon casting the ideal amount of light.

There were no people, no cars, and no other movement than the two of them in this moment.

Jonathan startled when his phone buzzed, and he heard an echo from hers. The cars were arriving. Hers came first, and he gave her a final kiss, one that heated his blood. He nearly didn't let her go, but the driver blared his horn. With another laugh, she pulled away, and he moved to open the door for her. His own Uber pulled up, the headlights illuminating her face.

"Thank you again," she said. "It was a wonderful day."

He walked to his car, greeting the driver, and climbing in. Suddenly the car in front, Breena's car, lurched to a stop and his Uber driver slammed on the brakes with a curse. Breena leapt out of the car and ran toward him.

"Wait," she shouted, her hair glowing in the headlights. "I almost forgot!"

nine

SABRINA UNLOCKED the door to her house and hung the keys on their hook. She leaned against the closed door, her hobo bag dangling from her fingers. She couldn't believe she'd nearly forgotten to get Johnny's phone number, especially after the amazing ... day ... dinner ... date or whatever it was they'd had. Had she truly met a random guy at the beach, gone out to dinner and a movie with him and then shared the most arousing kiss she'd ever had? Without even knowing his last name?

Thank god her Uber driver had listened when she'd yelled at him to stop. Especially because she and Johnny hadn't shared anything very personal during their date. He was a surfer who owned his own business, and he liked campy horror movies.

And she'd lied to him about who she was. Maybe that hadn't been such a good idea. But when she'd started the lie, she hadn't known he'd be such an amazing kisser. Or that she'd want to see him again.

She crossed into her family room, putting her bag into its place in the coat closet and flicking on lights as she went. This house was much smaller than the one she'd shared with her ex-husband, Leroy, but over the last year, she'd grown to love it. She liked only having one small space for relaxing, one that fit her needs with a comfortable couch, an armchair perfect for reading in, and a TV if she ever felt the urge to stream a show.

Besides, up until recently, she'd rarely used the family room. When she'd been working for Thinkfling she'd come home, order takeout or grab a pre-made salad, and go directly into her office to fight her way through emails, SWOTs, A3s, and various projects. If she felt lonely, she'd play some Brandi Carlile or Patty Griffin or stream a trashy TV show in the background.

Sabrina looked around the room, feeling like she was seeing it for the first time. There was nothing on the walls, no rugs over the hardwood floors, not even a dying orchid sitting on a windowsill. It was like a minimalistic hotel room, lacking personality; bland and boring. It lacked her personality—she wasn't bland and boring.

Right?

Right!

She should do some shopping, add some tasteful prints, maybe a cozy blanket for the couch, perhaps a small bookshelf for books to go under the TV. She didn't normally buy paperbacks, maybe she could start. Perhaps Johnny would want to come by, cuddle under the blanket with her and watch some campy horror movie while explaining to her that the blood and gore were actually a commentary on societal issues and that horror always got more popular when societal things were tough. Like they were now. Horror hadn't been a genre of movie she'd ever enjoyed, but the way Johnny broke it down and analyzed it was interesting. She should watch some of the movies he'd recommended, see if they could talk more about them at a future date.

Her phone buzzed. Was it Johnny already? Didn't that break some dating rule?

LYING, BAKING, & SURFING

Pulling her phone out of a pocket, she read the screen. Just a text notification of a sale at a professional clothing store. Texting the word "stop", she went to close the app, but paused.

She wanted to text Johnny, just a thank you for a great evening, but even she knew it was too soon. But god, she wanted to. She hadn't felt this euphoria of potential, of romance, of really liking another person since high school. Not even Leroy had made her feel this giddy and high on life.

Getting a cup of tea—at least she did share that enjoyment with Breena—she settled onto the couch for some social media stalking of Johnny now that she had his last name. She started with LinkedIn. Nothing; but a lot of small businesses didn't have LinkedIn profiles, so no surprise. Then she checked Twitter—nothing. Well, that might be an indication of his political leanings, which was a point in his favor. Then she tried Instagram. Nothing. She frowned and put down her teacup. Had she spelled his last name wrong? She flipped back to her contacts. He'd entered his name as Johnny Delgado; he shouldn't have misspelled it—it was pretty common. She even struck out on Facebook, though she did find out her ex-husband had recently gotten a puppy, thanks to his new girlfriend.

She took a sip of tea, pushing down emotions she didn't want to analyze, and focused back on Johnny. Maybe he'd given up on social media. That might be something to aspire to; there were so many studies that said how bad social media was for mental health. Maybe it was part of Johnny's surfer attitude. She'd have to ask him.

Her phone buzzed.

> Hey! Can you call me? I have a quick question, and it's too hard to ask via text.

God, it was like Leroy always knew when she'd been thinking about him.

> What if I'm busy?

> You're not. You haven't updated your LinkedIn, so I know you're not putting in crazy hours at some new job.

Their divorce hadn't been heated. There'd been a few fights leading up to it, but their marriage had been over years before they'd signed the papers. But it had still hurt. The worst part was he'd requested the divorce for the right reason; she worked too much, and he'd felt ignored. Looking back, she wasn't even sure if she'd ever really loved him. It had just been easier to marry him than keep dating, easier to have someone to come home to, easier than trying to date and manage a career.

Sabrina changed into pajamas, purchased a large cuddle blanket online (available tomorrow!), made herself a second cup of chamomile tea, and asked her Alexa to play some jazz.

Her phone buzzed.

> I'm going to head to bed if you're not going to call, and it's pretty important I talk to you.

Sabrina sighed and pressed the phone icon.

ten

"WHAT'S GOING ON?" Sabrina asked her ex-husband.

"What took you so long?" Leroy asked, his voice slightly tinny over her phone. "What were you up to?"

"Just settling down for the night. About to head to bed." She picked at a small spot on her couch. Maybe she should get a cat for company. Or a fish. They were less work.

"What'd you need?" she asked.

"I can't find my cast-iron skillets. I thought I had them, but I don't. We had five, remember? And I can't find a single one."

Of course she remembered the cast-iron skillets. She'd accidentally washed one, scrubbing it until it was clean, after she'd missed her nephew's birthday party—emergency brunch meeting with the executives to talk about nothing that actually mattered. Leroy had been pissed, and she'd tried to make it up to him by cleaning the kitchen, but apparently, you weren't supposed to use dish soap on cast-iron skillets. Or a wire brush.

He'd gone to a hotel that night.

"I can't find them anywhere," Leroy continued. "I bet you have them in a box you haven't opened, or your movers put them away and you never noticed."

Sabrina took a sip of tea, hoping the chamomile would live up to its advertising for calmness, before responding. "We moved out of the house on Seagull Drive over a year ago. You didn't need them before this moment?"

"I kept thinking they'd turn up."

"Well, they haven't."

"You aren't going to use them," he snapped.

"Of course not," she responded, fighting to keep her voice calm. She wasn't going to start an argument with Leroy. Not after the fun evening she'd had with Johnny. "If I had them, I'd return them."

He let out a giant sigh. Then another. She could almost hear him counting in his head. "Sorry," he said. "I know you would. I'm just trying to make this macaroni-and-cheese that needs a cast-iron skillet and can't find any of them. We're doing a recipe contest with my family. Remember those?"

She did; the Saturday nights when his brothers, sister, and parents would compete for the best cornbread, or hamburger, or once an entire turkey dinner. They'd sit around with wine or beer, and eat so much their stomachs would hurt, declare a winner, and play some silly board game past midnight. Leroy's siblings had never moved far from their home, and his parents had simply adopted all the spouses, partners, and kids. Every year it felt like birthdays and Thanksgivings just got larger and louder, with lots of wine, laughter, and do-you-remember memories. But naturally she'd stopped being invited to their family events after the divorce. And if she was being honest, she'd skipped out on a lot of the family get-togethers anyway, prioritizing work and assuming she'd always make the next one.

Whelp, that plan hadn't worked out.

With what felt like a punch to her chest, she realized she missed his family, missed their craziness. The holidays would come, and she wouldn't have anyone to spend them with, and no work to use as an excuse. She took a breath trying to calm her heart, push down the pain. The holidays were still several months away and nothing to worry about now. She needed to control what she could.

"Sabrina? You there?"

"Of course. Sorry, I must be getting tired and zoned out for a second there. I'll check the boxes in the garage in the next few days."

"Ok. Let me know. We're competing this weekend and I can order another one, but the really good ones, like what we had, are like three hundred dollars."

"I'll look tomorrow when I'm home from work," she promised.

"Oh congrats," he said. "Where are you working? That must be a relief; I can't imagine you not having a job."

She shouldn't have said anything. She rubbed at the spot on the couch again, wondering what had caused the stain; she didn't normally eat on the couch.

"The job's nothing big," she said. "Just something to keep me busy until . . . ." She didn't know what came next. Until she found something else? Doing what?

"What's your new job?" She heard him pour a drink, the clink of ice in the glass.

She didn't want to tell him. But she wasn't going to lie either. "I work at a bakery," she said. "I knead the dough and shape it and mix the ingredients. And lately, work the counter."

"Right," he said with a chuckle. "Totally see you doing that."

"I'm serious," she said.

"Wait—you really work at a bakery?" His incredulity was palatable, even over the phone. "You? You're messing with me."

"No. I like it." She kept her voice boardroom calm; he was beginning to annoy her. The job at the bakery wasn't the mindless task she'd been aiming for, but she liked the physical act of making something from scratch. Something that brought people joy.

"Kneading dough? You? You hate cooking!"

"I'm actually enjoying it." Her hands were starting to shake with anger. She took another sip of tea, trying to take a subtle deep breath. She would not fight with her ex-husband. It was pointless.

"Ok, now I'm worried," Leroy said. "I mean, I know we . . . you know, but . . . you have a minimum wage job at a bakery? You're one of the smartest, most confident, bad-ass business bitches I know."

Sabrina winced. She used to write "bad-ass business bitch" in the steam on mirrors, on scrap paper, in her notes on her phone when she needed the boost. Of course Leroy had spotted it.

"You wanted to be the CEO of Thinkfling," Leroy continued. "Had a three-year plan on the board in your office and everything."

"Plans change," she snapped.

"But people don't. I don't know, hon, maybe you need some therapy or something."

"It's not like I'm stripping and dancing around a pole," she said. "Or playing a guitar for tips on a street corner. Or hiding in my bed, refusing to get up. Or sitting on the couch and day-drinking while binging Netflix. I'm getting out there and trying something."

"I know, I know," he murmured. She could almost see him standing in the kitchen, running his hands through his hair. "Look, I'm going to text you the name of my therapist. He's really helped me since the divorce, figuring things out."

"I'm fine." She slammed her teacup down onto the coffee table, the hot liquid sloshing onto the wood.

"I know you think you are," he said soothingly, the way he used to when he'd tell her how much she'd disappointed him by putting her job before him. "I mean, I'm just worried."

"I'm fine," she said again. "In fact, I just had the best day. Just went with whatever was going to happen. I didn't even freak out when my car got locked in the parking lot. It was outside of my control, so I let it go."

"What happened? Do you need me to call a locksmith? Drive you somewhere?"

God, sometimes he was just too nice. Too accommodating. Too helpful.

"I'm good. Just forgot the beach parking lot closed at sundown. I took an Uber home, and I'll take another one in the morning to get my car. It'll be fine in the parking lot."

"You forgot. You? Forgot? See, this is what I'm talking about. I mean, you would miss stuff, but you didn't forget about them. You forgetting your car in a lot that closed at sundown is not like you. You automatically check for that type of thing and would never let your car get locked up. And if it did, you'd be huffing and puffing—"

"I would not. That's horribly insulting!"

Leroy took another deep breath. "You would be frustrated, you have to admit. Seriously, Sabrina, you need to see a therapist. You need to process your emotions, not push them down." She heard a voice in the background, a female one, and then his muffled response to her. Must be the new girlfriend. The one he'd gotten a puppy with.

"Ok, I gotta go," Leroy said. "Do you need help getting your car?"

"I'm fully capable of taking an Uber to my car," she tried not to snap.

He let out a puff of air, obviously counting again. "Ok then. Please look for those skillets."

It was hard to know which of them hung up first.

What an asshole, telling her what she was or wasn't! She could be a baker if she wanted. He didn't control her. He never had.

Sabrina cleaned up the mess from the tea and went into her home office. She hadn't been in here since being fired. There was still a sticky note on her computer screen reminding her of a work task she'd never complete and the CEO obviously hadn't cared about her completing at all.

Her three-year plan to become the CEO of Thinkfling was attached to one white board, another had a list of projects and which of her direct reports were handling them. In this room, she'd paced, cried, and done fist-pumps when everything had worked out. She'd sent emails from here at midnight when she couldn't sleep and at four a.m. when she'd gotten up early to complete an important assignment. So many plans and ideas were brainstormed and completed in this room.

For a company that had let her go when she wasn't meeting their expectations, which she still didn't understand.

For a company she'd gotten a divorce for.

For a company she hadn't had children for.

For a company who had turned her into an executive, not as a job title, but as a way of being.

Who was she if she wasn't a VP for Thinkfling? A laidback yoga instructor, like she'd pretended with Johnny? Yeah right. She liked the yoga classes she attended, but her promise to do them every day from YouTube videos hadn't manifested. If she was being honest, the meditation part of the yoga classes drove her crazy, and she wasn't super bendy and beautiful like the people in the class were.

She actually kind-of hated yoga.

Sabrina ran her fingers through her hair, poking at her emotions. She didn't hate yoga, she clarified with herself. There were parts she liked. She liked the feel of her muscles moving in new ways, the focus on breathing, and how calm her mind was afterwards. She liked the few seconds when her thoughts went silent.

Sitting down in her desk chair, she spun in a slow circle. She was a planner and a strategic thinker. Leroy was right. She wasn't a baker or the yoga instructor, Breena she'd pretended to be with Johnny. She wasn't someone who met a random person, went to the movies, and then made out with him on the beach. It had been freeing to pretend to be someone else, but she'd been pretending. That wasn't fair to Johnny. And when she thought about it, it was kind of embarrassing.

God, she didn't know who she was. Was she a bad-ass business bitch? Who was Sabrina if she didn't have Thinkfling, or a family, or even friends? Could she be Breena if she tried hard enough? Did she want to be?

At Thinkfling, she'd made nearly a quarter of a million dollars annually. The mortgage on her house in Encinitas, close to the beach was ridiculous, her Tesla had a high monthly payment and furnishing this house, even as minimally as she had, had made a huge dent in her savings. Her minimum wage salary as a baker wasn't enough for her standard of living and she was bleeding money. San Diego was one of the most expensive places in the country to live and if she wanted to stay here, she was going to need to start making more money.

And being a baker, doing nothing but kneading dough, was wasting her talents. She'd spent a fortune on education, on seminars, and on leadership books. She knew what she was doing and knew how to run a company. It was time to focus and put her life back together. What had she been thinking, going to dinner and the movies with Johnny when her life was such a mess? Romance shouldn't be in the cards, especially not with a surfer who thought she was someone named Breena. She wasn't a free-spirit. She was a bad-ass business bitch who started each day with a schedule, a to-do list, and priorities. And it was time to behave that way.

With a firm nod to herself, she pulled out her phone and began to text.

> It's Breena. I had the most incredible time tonight. I meant it when I said it was the best day of my life. Tears filled her eyes, but she kept typing. But I'm going through a lot right now and a romance isn't what's best for me. And I don't want to hurt you or make you think I'm available. I'm not. I'm so sorry.

She read it over and over, her finger hovering over "send."

eleven

JONATHAN SAT at his kitchen table in his condo, rereading the email from the sub for his sixth period class. And read it again. He'd been on such a high from his date with Breena, he should've known checking his work email would make it come crashing down. He should've just gotten up early in the morning, gotten his car, then gone into work, THEN checked his email.

Actually, he probably shouldn't have played hooky today. Then the sub wouldn't have screwed up with one of his more challenging students. Samuel, a freshman with undiagnosed neurodivergency, hadn't taken well to the sub's request that Samuel sit and read the history assignment quietly. Samuel had been... Samuel. He'd requested to go to the bathroom several times and when the sub had refused, he'd noisily drunk from his water bottle, then tapped his pen on his desk, "annoying" the students around him, according to the email.

Jonathan shook his head. He'd selected easy-going students around Samuel who wouldn't be bothered by his quirks until the team at the school could help the teenager become more self-aware. The sub had even mentioned that she hadn't allowed the student to chew gum, like she was proud of herself, when the chewing gum was a tactic he and the other teachers used with Samuel, and others like him, to help with focus.

The sub had finally had enough of the student's behavior and had sent the freshman to the office, mishandling the situation horribly. Getting in "trouble" and being sent to the office would humiliate and shut Samuel down. He wasn't a discipline problem like other students who thought being sent to the office was a reward.

Jonathan rubbed at the spot between his eyes. He shouldn't have taken the day off; shouldn't have gone surfing, shouldn't have gone to the movies with Breena. Students like Samuel and Lily needed him. They were his priority. Especially after he'd failed Lily, not seeing the signs of her depression. He couldn't be the free-spirit Breena was. He had work to do, and not just the grading he'd be awake until midnight working on.

He typed out a response to the sub, but "hey princess—take some classes on how to teach students with neurodivergence" didn't seem very professional. Instead, he closed the email program, planning to respond in the morning, and opened the grading program. Even if he just read through four or five of the essays, it would help him feel more caught up.

Putting on a classic rock station, he prepared to read about how Lincoln's choice to have Jackson as his vice president had changed America. Wrapping up one essay (83%—nice job!) he got up to get a glass of water, his eyes falling on his vintage Creature of the Black Lagoon poster. His ex-girlfriend had hated his posters. Actually, she'd hated his condo and wanted him to redecorate with less "dorm room" art. He wondered how they'd lasted the two years they had. He'd been nuts to take Breena, the laid-back bohemian he'd just met, to the movie marathon. It usually took several dates before he admitted to his love for campy horror movies and Star Wars.

But despite her relaxed way of looking at the world, Breena had liked the movies. And she hadn't made fun of his love for Star Wars, either. He bent over to pet his black lab, Lando. The dog opened one eye and thumped his tail at Jonathan. "Do you think Breena would like you? I think she just might. She's pretty cool."

Lando didn't respond, just yawned, and thumped his tail again. Jonathan returned to his grading, eyes drooping, but promising to finish the essay he was on.

A text message buzz interrupted his focus. It was almost midnight. Had Breena texted him already? Didn't she know that broke the dating rules? But maybe she was so easygoing, she didn't care. He'd never met a woman so confident in living with whatever life put in front of her.

His heart leaping, he began to read the message.

> It's Breena. I had the most incredible time tonight. I meant it when I said it was the best day of my life. But I'm going through a lot right now and a romance isn't what's best. And I don't want to hurt you or make you think I'm available. I'm not. I'm so sorry.

Like the email from the sub, he had to read it repeatedly. His heart dropped into his stomach; that hadn't been the response he'd been expecting, especially after their kiss and her running back to him for his phone number. He thought they'd had a great time. He thought he'd see her again, at least. And he'd already planned all the delicious things they'd do in bed together.

Maybe she hadn't been as into the movies as he'd thought. Maybe she'd already met someone else. Maybe she'd gone back to her place with the Uber driver or been to another bar and met someone there. She was relaxed, so relaxed that she'd spent the day with him, someone she didn't even know.

Maybe this was what dating someone like her was like; up one minute, down the next.

> But we had so much fun.

Delete.

> You made me feel alive.

Delete.

> Please don't. Whatever I did wrong, I can fix it.

Delete.

> I understand. I had a great time tonight, but I get it. If you change your mind and want to grab coffee, or see another monster movie, just send a text.

His finger hovered over "send", rereading the message, waiting to see if the three dots would appear and she'd text, *just kidding,* or *I changed my mind,* or *I've been attacked by zombies and one of them sent the text.*

When it didn't appear, when there was no other response, he hit send.

twelve

SABRINA HAD A PLAN:

1. Quit the bakery.
2. Speak to a financial planner about her savings and portfolio.
3. Put together a tight budget that didn't include dinners out at hole-in-the-wall Italian places until she started to bring in some sustainable income.
4. Put together a package for consulting with small businesses on their marketing.
5. Within two weeks, start putting out feelers for consulting work.
6. Find balance between going with the flow and being a bad-ass business bitch.
7. Never go back to Moonlight Beach.

Time for number one. She walked into Sugar Bliss, a fantastic sunrise beginning to paint the sky with pinks and purples. The bell chimed behind her. Hattie was already inside, the expresso maker hissing and churning, the smell of coffee, flour, sugar, and apple in the air.

Sabrina always marveled at how Hattie was there before she was—ready for the day—and then staying after Sabrina left. But she'd also seen the joy, the peace on Hattie's face when the other woman mixed dough, kneading, and folding it to the perfect consistency. Then shaping the creations, tucking them into the oven and pulling the perfectly baked masterpieces out of the heat. Hattie was a true artist who loved the baking side of her business but hated the actual business part. It was a testament to Hattie's skill that Sugar Bliss had survived as long as it had.

Sabrina tied on her apron and eyed the crates of granny smith apples against the back door of the kitchen. "Are we making pies?"

"Better," Hattie said. "I got a great deal on these so we're making my special recipe of apple coffeecake with a thick caramel drizzle. I made this two years ago and word got out. We sold them all in an hour."

"Sounds yummy," Sabrina said.

"Yeah, I was thinking about something you said about taking things to the next level."

"I did?"

"Something about using social media—which wouldn't work—but my special recipes do. I don't know how it happens, but people get out there and tell everyone about these. We'll sell these for $21.99."

"That much?" Sabrina said. "I mean, I know we're in Encinitas and it's all tourists, but—"

"Trust me," Hattie said. "These are going to make all the difference. Word will get out and we'll—anyway. Word will get out." But the other woman frowned and swallowed hard. Something was going on.

"I believe you," Sabrina said, her voice gentle. "But I also need to tell you something."

Hattie handed Sabrina a mug of coffee, doctored with the perfect amount of cream and sugar, the word "patience" painted across the china. Sabrina stared at the word. Why would Hattie give her a random mug with that word? Was the universe trying to tell her something? That couldn't be a coincidence.

She took a deep breath. Maybe she should wait before quitting her job at Sugar Bliss. She wouldn't run out of money in the next few days—heck, she probably had six months if she was careful with her money. She had the time and the privilege to build her consulting plan after work in the evenings while avoiding Moonlight Beach. Maybe the universe was telling her to be patient and just go with the flow.

"Never mind," she told Hattie. "Let's get to work. I can't wait to try these coffee cakes."

"Great," Hattie said. "Start peeling and chopping."

Two hours later, she and Hattie had created forty disposable tins full of the coffee cake, some ready for customers to wrap up and take home, others ready for slices to be cut from and eaten on the spot. Hattie sliced into a cake and offered Sabrina a sliver. Sabrina's eyes closed of their own accord as butter, cinnamon, and sugar hit her tongue, followed by the sweet apple. She almost lunged for the rest of the cake.

Hattie laughed, her good humor restored with the simple act of baking. "I'll wrap one up for you if you'll do me a favor."

"Sure," Sabrina said, brushing crumbs from her fingers. There was something tangible and pleasant about looking around and seeing all she'd done. Sure, her shoulders and wrists ached from mixing and pouring, but they'd always ached after working a twelve-hour day on a computer in her previous life.

"Can you stay after your six hours, just for eight hours today?" Hattie asked. "Cloey won't be coming in. You'd have to take a lunch, but . . ."

"I can make that work. Is Cloey ok?"

"Oh yeah," Hattie said, breaking eye contact and staring over Sabrina's shoulder. "She just needs to focus on school right now."

"Uh huh," Sabrina said, her years of office politics helping her see through the lie.

Hattie sighed. "I keep forgetting you came from corporate. No one can lie to you."

"They have to be really good at it. What's actually going on?"

"I can't afford her right now," Hattie said, running her fingers through her graying hair, then going to the sink to wash them again. "I need more help with the baking than I do at the counter, and she can't come in early. And you're cheaper."

"You know," Sabrina said. "If I may . . . I think there are some things you can do to save money. Even just using an inventory program for your ingredients and stock might help. I know we donate a fair amount of our inventory at the end of the day, and that's wonderful, but have you thought—"

"My system works fine," Hattie said, cutting her off. "Our leftover stock sent to Father Joe's Villages makes a difference in someone's life. This way I know children can get a sweet treat, maybe a peaceful moment, when they're going through hell. Let's get everything else made. We have a lot of work and need to open in an hour."

Sabrina dutifully mixed the daily cinnamon rolls, putting them in the oven to rise and then moving on to crumpets, sticky buns, and loafs of wheat bread thick with seeds. She mixed, kneaded, and poured. Focusing on the moment, she tried to think of nothing more than the feel of dough beneath her hands and knuckles, the smell of baking and finding satisfaction in creating baked goods; goods so good Hattie often had a few people waiting when she unlocked the front door.

But she couldn't push past the familiar ache of frustration. She was good at her previous job; she knew marketing and how to save companies money. Hattie should listen to her. The bakery owner could double her profits and hire many Cloeys in just a few months. But the other woman was too set in her ways to listen to Sabrina.

Maybe the "patience" on the coffee cup had been for Hattie, not for Sabrina, and the universe had gotten the message confused. Sabrina probably needed to return to her original plan of quitting this job and focusing on consulting.

At seven a.m., Sabrina unlocked the door while Hattie slid the last of the trays into the glass display case. She greeted the first customer, an older woman, who walked the few blocks to the bakery, buying her bread for the day, before walking back home to put her feet up. The woman was pleased to see the coffee cake, buying two.

But by nine, they'd only sold a few more cakes to the regulars; Hattie's promised stampede of customers hadn't come. The owner kept wandering out of her office to tweak the display.

"Do you want me to put up a sign?" Sabrina finally asked when there were still thirty of the cakes left. "Perhaps that will get some tourist walking by to stop."

"Sure," Hattie said with a shrug, going back into her office and closing the door behind her.

Sabrina got out a piece of paper and a sharpie but had an idea.

She arranged a few of the coffee cakes on a pretty wooden tray and snapped a few pictures with her phone.

"Actually," Sabrina asked, going into Hattie's office and

disturbing the other woman shopping for used baking paraphernalia on eBay. "Can I use your computer and create a pretty sign with a picture?"

"With a picture?"

"Yeah," she showed Hattie the pictures she'd taken of the cakes with the effect of steam rising she'd added with a filter.

Hattie rolled out of the way with a grunt. "I guess."

Within five minutes, Sabrina had elegant flyers advertising the coffee cake. She hung one on the front door. "Can't hurt," she told Hattie.

More time went by with no cakes being sold, and Sabrina jumped onto social media. She didn't just post pictures of the cakes on her personal pages; instead she stalked all the local community pages, posting pictures of the coffee cake and the bakery. Wincing, she even posted fake reviews, exclaiming how amazing the bakery and these unique coffee cakes were.

It worked.

Within an hour, the bell jingled again and again, people from the local neighborhood who hadn't been in for years, buying the cakes, plus sticky buns, and cinnamon rolls, exclaiming over how long it had been since they'd last stopped by Sugar Bliss and yet Hattie and the bakery hadn't changed.

At one point, there were so many customers, Hattie came out to help wrap up the purchases, smiling at all the compliments and greeting customers she hadn't seen in forever. They sold out of the coffee cake by noon and Sabrina had to hang another sign on the door telling people they were out, but to please come in and buy something else.

"I can't believe that sign worked," Hattie said during a break between customers.

"It helped," Sabrina said. "But I also used all the local Facebook pages and posted a ton on Instagram. I just reminded them you were still here."

Hattie sniffed.

"I can help you create your own Instagram page," Sabrina continued. "We can offer giveaways and punch cards, encouraging people to post their pictures and experiences. Get you a fresh coat of paint on the walls, updated art, and some window—"

Hattie went into her office and slammed the door.

Whoops. Sabrina had gone too far. She rubbed her forehead. She used to be better at this. But her previous clients had hired Thinkfling and were open to ideas and changes. Hattie just wasn't.

Her ideas were good, right?

Maybe they weren't. Maybe had lost her touch. Maybe Thinkfling had been right to fire her.

Butterflies of anxiety rose in her stomach, and she pushed them down. God, maybe she should just quit everything and become a bum living on the beach. But the beach made her think of Johnny. Unable to resist, she pulled out her phone. She reread his response to her break-up text.

Maybe she'd been too hasty with Johnny. One date wasn't a relationship. Maybe she should ask him out for coffee, take things slow and see where they went.

The bell chimed, and Sabrina looked up.

"Nixi!" she said. "You found me."

"You're posting all over Facebook about some place called Sugar Bliss with amazing coffee cake," her former assistant said. "Of course I found you. When are you off? I got something to tell you!"

thirteen

SABRINA SIPPED on her craft cocktail flavored with lavender while waiting for Nixi at Boundaries in La Jolla. A speakeasy hidden behind a secret door in the corner of a restaurant, Boundaries was one of Sabrina's favorite bars. The owners had taken the idea of a speakeasy and run with it, decorating with a tin-tiled ceiling, old family pictures on the walls, and a dim interior lit by flickering lamps. An old-fashioned bar with black velvet bar stools and a foggy mirror completed the 1920s mystic. Sabrina adored the atmosphere. The bartenders were fun to watch as they mixed different liquors and mixers together, shaking, stirring, and pouring them into various cocktail glasses over ice. The smell of cedar smoke from smoked drinks and singed oranges filled the air.

She closed her eyes, trying to be in the moment, trying to enjoy the modernized 1920s music playing, the surrounding smells, and the murmur of conversation. She'd always missed out on these moments of doing "nothing" when she worked at Thinkfling, always rushing to the next meeting or project. In the past, she would've been working on emails from her phone while waiting for her friend. But now she could just sit and watch the other diners sip their cocktails and enjoy charcuterie boards full of interesting cheeses and meats.

Annnndddd . . . one minute later, she was back on her phone, scrolling through random social media apps without having made the conscious decision to pick up her phone. She missed the constant pinging of people needing her, of emails and Teams messages to read. She missed the adrenaline and the feeling of being needed. What did that say about her?

She dropped her head into her hands with a faint groan. Then she sat up, turned her phone so it was face down, and made a concerted effort to look around. She watched a young couple take a seat in a booth, scooting next to each other and pointing out various items on the menu. She observed a group of women sitting at the bar laugh about something on one of their phones as they passed it around. Someone returned a drink to the bartender, complaining it was too strong and requesting a drink with less rum.

Her hand moved back to her phone and before she realized it, she was scrolling through previous texts. Nothing from Nixi saying she was running late. Her eyes fell on the last message from Johnny.

> I understand. I had a great time tonight, but I get it. If you change your mind and want to grab coffee, or see another horror movie, just send a text.

God, his response to her break-up text was perfect, too. She'd really liked him. Though he'd only liked the person she'd pretended to be. Not the neurotic mess she actually was. A relationship was out of the question until she figured herself out.

"So, Thinkfling is falling apart without you," Nixi said as a greeting as she pulled out the bar stool next to Sabrina and sat down. Sabrina watched her friend flick her dark, braided hair over her shoulders. The bartender, a red-headed woman with tattoos up and down her arms, came over to take Nixi's order. The other woman ordered a cocktail with a champagne base and a mushroom flatbread. "No one knows what to do without you," Nixi continued. "I mean honestly. We're about to lose the Barajas account."

Pain punched Sabrina in the chest, harder than she would've expected, making her gasp. She covered it by taking a sip of her cocktail and then drained the glass. Acquiring the Barajas account, an international company selling cold-pressed green drinks, had taken her six months of meetings, presentations, and proposals. She believed Barajas's drinks could have a place in the San Diego markets, with the right marketing strategy.

That she had designed.

All of her hard work was about to be undone. By a bunch of idiots who cared more about profits and their own egos, than in helping the companies who paid Thinkflings's bills.

But the execs at Thinkfling hadn't cared about her. She shouldn't care about them either.

"Good," Sabrina said as firmly as she could. "Good," she said again, pushing down the pain in her chest. "I'm the one who built those relationships, catered to their egos, knew what they wanted."

"You truly were." Nixi took a sip from her cocktail, her tiny nose stud glinting in the lights from the bar. "They're freaking out about losing the account, but they ruined the relationship with one stupid email."

Nixi had been Sabrina's personal assistant for over five years, and they'd developed a close friendship. The other woman knew where everything was at Thinkfling, knew everyone, maintained Sabrina's calendar and list of to-dos, and had a fun sense of humor. She'd held Sabrina's hand during Sabrina's divorce, placating the other executives when Sabrina needed a few extra minutes to rant or cry.

"So what happened? How did they ruin the Barajas account?" Sabrina asked.

"Don't know. That info's not part of the gossip. But it must have been a massive screw-up."

She didn't care; she didn't care; she didn't care.

A server delivered Nixi's flatbread and Sabrina's designer burger. Sabrina bit in, relishing the flavors of pickles, bacon, and onion jam. And the best part, the meat. Even if she figured out yoga and meditation, she'd never be able to give up meat.

"So they thought they'd promote Orson into your position—"

"What?!" Sabrina shouted, nearly knocking over her empty cocktail glass. "He has no critical thinking skills. He makes pretty spreadsheets, and that's about it."

"Exactly," Nixi said. "And he talks a good talk." Sabrina raised an eyebrow. "He does," Nixi said, finishing half of her cocktail in one long sip. "He's very eloquent. But anyways, he refused."

"What?" Sabrina shouted again, getting an odd look from the bartender.

"Yeah," Nixi continued. "Orson said he thought your old job was too much for one person."

"He didn't!"

"And that he would call you. He wants to know where you went, so he can follow you."

Sabrina's heart warmed, the pain in her chest receding. "That's very nice of him." She dipped a fry in the aioli sauce poured into a little ramequin.

"So, how's it really going?" Nixi asked after the bartender checked in on them, and they both refused a second drink. "I like your new look."

Today Sabrina had worn a loose tank top that told everyone to "breathe" and leggings with a short flowery skirt over the top. "I've always been envious of people who dressed this way, so I thought I'd try it."

"And it looks good on you, too. It suits you." Nixi reached over to straighten Sabrina's beaded necklace, her hand pausing. "It shouldn't suit you, though," Nixi said, cocking her head to the side. "But it does."

"Thank you. I've started doing some yoga," Sabrina said. "And my instructor has this book on letting go of things you can't control and being present. I'm trying to think about life and all the little stressors differently."

"I'm so impressed with you," Nixi said. "I would still be hiding on the couch under a blanket, day-drinking and binge-watching Netflix."

"I tried that. It was boring."

"Is that why you got the job at that bakery? I didn't think you liked cooking."

Sabrina stopped to take another bite of her burger, licking a bit of onion jam off a finger. "Partially. I just wanted to do something, make something tangible, I guess. But . . ." she grimaced. "I'm not sure how long it'll last." She told Nixi all about the apple coffee cake that morning and Hattie's reaction to her social media posts. "The owner is just set in her ways, and doesn't want to change, even if it's working," she concluded. "But because of what I did, we sold out of those coffee cakes and sold so many other buns and rolls, too. Some of those people hadn't been into Sugar Bliss in years. We'll get more customers from my social media posts than from anything the owner has done. But Hattie doesn't like it. Won't even listen! And I know what I'm doing. I'm good at marketing."

"You are," Nixi soothed. "The best of the best and a bad-ass business bitch." The other woman pursed her lips. "But it sounds like . . ." she paused. "It sounds like you're trying to control things outside your control."

Sabrina groaned. "I just want to help. But maybe you're right. This is a huge change for me, and I need to focus. Especially if she doesn't want my help." She tucked her hair behind her ears. "Besides I have this whole plan to open up my own consulting business. I need to—wait. What's going on?"

Nixi's attention was on the speakeasy's doorway, and not on what Sabrina was saying.

"Oh, my college ex just came in." Nixi turned back to Sabrina, her eyes firm on Sabrina's.

"College? You look lovely, by the way." Sabrina flicked one of Nixi's braids over her shoulder.

"Do you think he saw me?" Nixi asked, not looking away from Sabrina or changing her half-smile.

Sabrina glanced over Nixi's shoulder and met the eyes of the handsome Asian man standing at the door. He was watching them and gave an awkward half wave. Not knowing what to do, Sabrina waved back. "Oh yeah," she said, barely moving her lips. "He just waved at me, but I think he meant it for you. How'd your relationship end?"

"Fine," Nixi said. "I mean it wasn't a screaming, yelling fight or anything. He just said it was time to move on."

"He broke your heart."

"He did," Nixi said with a quick nod. "I've—"

"Coming over, coming over," Sabrina said under her breath. She took a bite of a fry.

"Nixi? I thought that was you," the man said, approaching them.

Nixi turned around on her barstool. "Oh my gosh! It's Kaito," she said, fooling no one.

He grinned, leaned close like he was going to hug her, then

turned it into a handshake when Nixi didn't move quick enough, then transformed it back into a hug. It was one of the more awkward things Sabrina had ever seen and she had to fight to keep from chuckling.

"Long time," Kaito said, standing between the two of them. "What are you up to?"

"Work, life, living by the ocean," Nixi said. "You?"

"Teaching math to high schoolers, believe it or not." He pushed his glasses up his nose. "Just moved back to the area, been here a few months. Been trying to connect with old friends. Didn't know you were still here."

"Never left," Nixi said, smoothing her fingers over the rim of her nearly empty cocktail glass.

Sabrina had never understood why that gesture showed flirting, but somehow it did. She'd tried it once on a date after her divorce and had knocked her drink into the guy's lap.

Thinking of dating made her think of Johnny and she carefully pushed the reminder away. That was over and done with.

Maybe Nixi could teach a seminar for divorcees on flirting. Sabrina could be her first client.

"Oh, this is my friend, Sabrina," Nixi said, introducing the two of them. "We're just having a quick drink."

"Did you want to join us?" Sabrina asked, resigning herself to being the awkward third wheel for the rest of the afternoon.

"I'm meeting a friend," Kaito said. "We're catching a movie in about thirty minutes." He glanced toward the doorway and waved.

Johnny?

fourteen

WHELP, *this was super awkward,* Sabrina thought. Less than twenty-four hours ago, she'd had one of the best dates of her entire life, culminating with a steamy make-out session in a beach parking lot, and a strong desire to drag Johnny back to her bed. And hours after that, she'd sent him a text, essentially breaking up with him.

She'd been trying to never think of him again.

And now he was standing in front of her.

The universe really was an asshole.

She pushed down her frustration. This was completely outside her control. She needed to let it go.

"Hey Johnny," she said to the surfer. "Small world." God, she was such an idiot. She'd already almost forgotten how good looking he was with his blonde hair and blue-green eyes that seemed to stare through her.

Nixi raised an eyebrow and looked back and forth between Sabrina and Johnny. "Hi!" she said, holding out her hand to Johnny when it was obvious no one was going to introduce them. "I'm Nixi, I used to work—"

"She and I are old friends," Sabrina jumped in. Nixi's

eyebrow went even higher. "This is Johnny," she told Nixi. "I met him yesterday at the beach. We had a great time chatting and then went out to dinner."

"This is Bre—" Johnny tried to tell Kaito.

"We just met!" Kaito spoke over him.

Silence fell and then kept stretching until the bartender came over to ask if the guys wanted a drink. Sabrina tried to subtly toss her napkin over her burger. If asked, she'd just say it was a meatless burger . . . and the bacon was . . . yeah . . . maybe he wouldn't see it.

"You're welcome to join us," Nixi said. "We can go grab one of the booths and chit-chat. Long as it's ok with you," she said to Sabrina, her eyes begging Sabrina to be fine with it.

"Of course, that's fine," Sabrina said, her cheeks flaming. This was so much worse than she could've imagined. But what else was she going to say? God, what did Johnny think of her, after her break-up text? After making out with him and then saying she didn't want to see him again?

Kaito looked back and forth between Sabrina and Johnny, trying to assess the situation without asking. Sabrina could almost feel Nixi vibrating with questions.

Kaito pulled out his phone and frowned, obviously pretending to check the time. "We do have that movie we were going to catch. What time was that at?" Kaito said, fooling no one that he was giving Johnny a way out.

"It's pretty soon," Johnny said, like he was grabbing onto a lifeline. Sabrina's cheeks got even hotter. Guess she now knew what he thought of her. "And I got stuck in that traffic," Johnny continued, staring at one of the old-fashioned photos lining the walls and not at anyone else. "I don't think we have time for a drink. Sorry everyone. Next time."

Sabrina wanted to curl up into a ball and disappear. This was super embarrassing. He obviously didn't want anything to do with her. Maybe her text had come as a relief. Maybe she'd completely misread what had happened last night. Maybe she'd had garlic breath or had been a terrible kisser. Or maybe he'd realized that she'd been pretending to be someone she wasn't.

"Sounds good," Kaito said. "It was nice to meet you," he told Sabrina. "Will you both be around in a few hours? We can stop by after the movie."

Nixi shook her head. "I have a kickboxing class I can't miss. But can you put your number in my phone?" she asked. "It would be great to catch up."

"I'd like that," Kaito said, holding her eyes with his for a bit too long, before accepting her phone and punching in his contact info. Sabrina glanced at Johnny. He was watching her and gave her a small smile.

She smiled back, just a little quirk of the lips, and dropped her eyes.

Saying goodbye, the guys left.

"What the hell?" Nixi asked, turning to Sabrina.

"Sorry. I'm a sucky wingman."

"Not that. I still got his number. How did you know that guy?"

"God." Sabrina wanted another drink. "I met him yesterday." She explained how she'd stopped the seagulls from flying away with Johnny's sweatshirt and how a coffee date had turned into a movie marathon and then dinner. She didn't explain that she'd pretended to be Breena, a yoga instructor—that was just too embarrassing.

"Ok," Nixi said, finishing off the flatbread. "So, you had a date with him. Why the awkwardness? Did you sleep with him, and it was terrible or something?"

"No. It was perfect."

"Really?" Nixi half screamed. "God, you're really embracing

this new Sabrina. You're my new hero and you already were my hero." She high-fived Sabrina.

"I didn't sleep with him," Sabrina clarified. "But I did make-out with him. It was perfect. And then I got home, and Leroy called."

"Ah," Nixi said. She put her hand over Sabrina's. "And he was typical Leroy, wasn't he?"

"I guess. He just . . . told me I was behaving erratically getting the job at the bakery after getting fired from Thinkfling, and he's right. I am. But I'm trying to . . ." Her eyes filled with tears, surprising her.

"Oh sweetie," Nixi said, putting her arms around Sabrina and pulling her into a hug. "You're doing just fine. It's only been a few weeks since they fired you."

Sabrina closed her eyes, the tears falling onto her friend's shoulder. After a minute, she pulled away and wiped her eyes. The female bartender put a few extra napkins out and poured a vodka shot for Sabrina. "On the house," she said before moving away so Sabrina and Nixi could continue their conversation.

Sabrina smiled through her tears and wiped them away. "So anyway," she continued. "After I talked to Leroy, I sent a text telling Johnny that I needed to focus on me. And that's the truth." Well, it was the partial truth. Most of it at least. Why on earth had she pretended to be someone else?

"I'm sure it was," Nixi said. "I'm just proud you went out on a date with him. Totally unplanned. Good for you!"

"I had the best time." Pretending to be someone she wasn't. Her cheeks burned just thinking about it. The relationship was doomed from the beginning.

"Exactly. You're growing. You're changing. And it's hard and it hurts."

"I'm trying to live in the moment and let go of things I can't control."

"You're trying to listen to the universe," Nixi supplied, finishing off her flatbread pizza.

"Exactly," Sabrina said. "I was going to quit Sugar Bliss and then Hattie handed me a mug that said patience. So I waited. And now Johnny shows up here. What does that mean? Should I see if he wants to hang out again?" She tossed back the shot, gasping at the harsh liquor.

"Running into him doesn't have to mean anything," Nixi said. "Or it can mean that you're supposed to call him and have mind-blowing sex. It's up to you. You can control whether or not you text him. But I do think it's interesting that you ran into him. Maybe the universe is trying to tell you something."

"But Leroy is right, too. And he called me right after the date. I'm not behaving like me. What if I mess it up?" Would Johnny even like bad-ass business bitch Sabrina? Or did he prefer bohemian Breena?

"What if Thinkfling calls you up and offers you your job back? What if you win the lottery? What if you get food poisoning and die from your burger? You can't plan every possibility."

"I know, I know," Sabrina said.

"But I think give it some time. If he's right for you, he's not going anywhere if you think about things for a few days."

"I guess."

The Whistle Song from Kill Bill rang out and Nixi winced, pulling her phone out of her purse. She showed Sabrina Thomas's professional picture—the CEO of Thinkfling—filling the screen.

Nixi sighed. "Oh, I forgot to tell you. I got promoted to his admin assistant. No more money, but lots more hours," she said with an eyeroll. "Hang on." She held her phone up to her ear. "Hi there! Yes, I was working on that today. I should have it done by ten tom—yes, by eight tonight." Her eyes dropped to the bar. "I'll head back to the office and get to work on it." She hung up and tossed her phone back into her purse.

"Let me guess," Sabrina said, quirking her eyebrows. "He has an early morning meeting he needs some report for and wants to prepare for it tonight. So, your part needs to be done so he can get his done."

"Yep."

"He's famous for that. That's why I worked all those crazy hours sometimes. But I never made you pull the reports after you'd gone home."

"Yeah. Have I told you how much I miss you?" She gave Sabrina a hug, threw a few bills down, and was gone before Sabrina could tell her to keep her money.

She watched her friend leave, a part of her missing those frantic phone calls that always gave her an excuse not to go home to either Leroy or her empty house. She missed having something to fill up her evenings.

But those evening calls from the executives demanding work had destroyed her marriage and her life. The other executives at Thinkfling were like her; divorced or on the brink of it. She was more than the job had forced her to become, damnit. She was more than an executive at Thinkfling.

Pulling out her phone, she deleted the LinkedIn app and pulled up her Facebook app. Anyone she wasn't close friends with were deleted. All those former clients and their partners she'd met at various events. Coworkers she hadn't talked to in years, former coworkers who'd moved on, she deleted them all. If they weren't like Nixi and they weren't friends outside of work, she deleted all of them.

She was done with Thinkfling. Done with the corporate experience. Done with letting others' expectations rule her life. She was going to choose who she wanted to be, even though she didn't know who that was yet.

LYING, BAKING, & SURFING

Ordering another drink, she looked at her phone. Her finger hovered over Johnny's icon.

Without thinking, without planning, she typed,

> Sooooooo.... I'm sorry. I think I was too hasty when I texted you last night. I've been regretting it all day. If that coffee is still available, I'd love to see you again. And I need to tell you something.

Her finger hovered over "send" then she hit delete until the only thing left was the *Soooooo....*

God, she was an idiot. She put the phone face down on the counter and canceled her drink order, asking for the bill.

fifteen

JONATHAN MOVED another unread email to the Outlook folder labeled, "Suicide Support Group." He didn't know why the parents were suddenly so angry about a teenager support group for survivors of suicide loss. It wasn't like he was running the group by himself—the school counselor was there, and the administration had approved it. And after Lily's death, he'd wanted to do something so her friends could grieve, so they could talk about her and the warning signs. For fuck-sake, he'd wished he'd seen the warning signs, too, just as much as her friends and family had.

But some parent had felt discussing suicide, even in a group about loss, would increase the likelihood of another teenager committing suicide. And it didn't seem to matter how many articles he and the school counselor sent home talking about how it didn't. Mentioning the word suicide didn't make kids suddenly contemplate it. Support groups like his actually helped to decrease suicide rates.

Though he had to admit, things had been ok until members from the LGBTQ+ club had started attending. It made sense; suicide rates were higher in the LGBTQ+ community than almost anywhere else, especially among teenagers and college students.

But that had been the final straw for this parent, and they had rallied up the community to demand his termination. These parents were dredging up off-hand comments he'd made in class, taking things out of context, using his lessons on the Holocaust and the Tulsa Massacre as further ammunition to demand he be fired.

God, this wasn't why he got into teaching history. He just wanted to help kids learn, increase their critical thinking skills, and think about what had happened in the past. He didn't want to deal with all this political drama from high school parents. Drama from high school kids was normal. Drama from high school parents shouldn't happen.

Turning off email notifications, he went back to entering grades into the school system. He didn't need any more angry emails from parents about being "behind" in his grading, too. Lando, his black lab, shifted position, his collar jingling. *Cabin in the Woods* played in the background, making him think of Breena. It was odd to think of her in terms of horror movies, but she'd seemed to enjoy *Army of Darkness* so much.

She'd been clearly embarrassed to see him yesterday at Boundaries, his favorite speakeasy in La Jolla. But he didn't know what that meant. She'd probably expected to never see him again, and then he turned up a day later. He hoped she didn't think he was stalking her. Luckily, Kaito had gotten there first, and the bar was right by the movie theatre.

And they hadn't stayed long. Just long enough for awkward small talk and for Nixi and Kaito to exchange phone numbers.

Jonathan picked up his phone and reread the last text between him and Sabrina, the one where he'd invited her to have coffee or see another movie if she changed her mind.

No new texts.

If she was going to change her mind, she would've texted him after seeing him yesterday, right? Or said more than just hi to him, avoiding eye contact and pretending to listen to Kaito and Nixi flirt.

She wasn't interested.
She wasn't interested.
She wasn't interested.
And he needed to get over it.
So, he typed out a text to Kaito.

> You got plans for this weekend? I want to surf again, and the waves are supposed to be good.

Kaito responded almost immediately.

> Can't. Too much grading.

> I get it. I'm entering grades now.

Jonathan paused before typing,

> Got more angry emails from parents.

> Dude. The parents are the worst part of this job.

> Yep.

Jonathan stood up and refilled his water.

> Why'd Nixi's friend call you Johnny? Meant to ask earlier. Did she rename you? Cuz that's not cool.

Jonathan wasn't going to explain how the name slipped out because he'd been pretending to be a surfer named Johnny.

> It just happened. Didn't bother me though. But it doesn't matter. She doesn't want to see me again anyway.

> You said that. Still don't know what you did?

> No clue. But whatever. It was just one date. Did you text Nixi again?

> Not yet. Might. A lot of history there. She was fun, though.

> Nothing wrong with fun.

Kaito liked the text, signaling the end of the conversation, and Jonathan went back to entering his grades. After he was done, he'd clean up the kitchen, walk Lando, and head to bed.

His phone buzzed, and he glanced down, his heart leaping. It was from Breena! She'd written,

> Soooooo....

He watched his phone for few minutes, but nothing else came through and there weren't any of the three dots indicating she was still typing.

What did "Soooooo...." mean? Was she saying she'd changed her mind? Was she waiting for him to respond? Did she want him to text back? Or should he wait a few days like she didn't matter?

What would surfer dude Johnny do? Jonathan thought about it and decided cool surfer Johnny would be sitting outside on his patio with a guitar, maybe smoking a little pot. He wouldn't be inside, grading papers, obsessing over an amazing, but frustrating woman. He shook the image away—marijuana was prevalent in San Diego, but not one of his vices.

He should wait a few days before responding at least. Be cool. After all, she was the one who'd broken things off with him. And her message was vague.

Another notification popped up on his phone; a calendar invite with the vice principal scheduled for tomorrow after classes. For fuck-sake, the parent complaints had reached the point where he needed to have a meeting with his boss? He'd quit if they canceled his suicide support group.

He texted the vice principal.

> How bad is it?

She responded immediately.

> Don't read and don't respond to any of those emails. The board, the administration, and myself in particular, support you, your support group, and what you're doing. We just need to coordinate our response.

Jonathan got up and got a beer from the fridge, taking a deep breath before typing,

> Coordinate our response?

> Don't worry.

> Keep doing what you're doing. We got your back.

This was ridiculous. He couldn't keep doing this. He wasn't happy.

LYING, BAKING, & SURFING

Without thinking, he pulled up another name and started typing.

> Hey, I don't know if you sent that text as an accident or what. But I could use some advice about how to control only what you can and let the rest go.

Without reading it, without thinking, he hit send.
And waited to see if Breena would respond.

sixteen

"I APPRECIATE IT MOM, TRULY," Sabrina said, putting the giant vase of flowers on her kitchen table and talking into her phone. "This delivery must have cost a fortune." She stroked a velvety rose. The arrangement was huge—full of perfectly bloomed orange dahlias, purple snapdragons, and soft pink roses. It had to be the most colorful arrangement Sabrina had ever received. "You didn't have to send flowers," she told her mother. "I'm fine."

"I thought you could use something cheerful," her mom said. "It's been a few weeks and if you're like me, after a big change, the adrenaline has worn off and I get depressed. Something small always helps."

Sabrina had always thought someone who owned a lingerie clothing line would be super feminine and sexy, with a trilling voice. Yet, her mother was anything but, keeping her hair short, her make-up light, and wearing pantsuits with sneakers. And her voice was fast and to the point. Whip-sharp even when she didn't mean it to be.

But her mother's lingerie company, named Beryl after the gemstone, focused on comfortable bras and no-show panties for working women. The bras were designed for all sizes, to prevent gapping and truly provide coverage and support. While expensive, her mother's company was all about helping those who couldn't afford bras, and they donated thousands of sets of underwear across the world.

So rather than being all about sex and power, her mother—Jacqueline—was about helping women in the workplace and through the different stages of womanhood. Her company even sold custom bras for women who had undergone partial mastectomies. And priced those according to what people could afford. She always said cancer was hard enough without having to worry about not being able to afford bras after losing a part of oneself.

A thought drifted across Sabrina's mind—she'd worked so hard at Thinkfling, trying to emulate her mother. But she'd chosen the wrong company to sacrifice everything for; one that cared more about profits than helping others. Tears sprung up in her eyes and she blinked them away.

"The flowers are there to brighten things up," Jacqueline continued. "I know you disagree, but the best thing I've ever done was to have flowers delivered both to my home and office weekly."

"I know, mom," Sabrina said wiping away tears and fighting to keep her voice normal. "They're lovely. And I appreciate the thought. What have you been up to lately?" she asked, hoping to distract her mother from more questions.

"I have to fly to Florida for a conference," her mother said. "I hate Florida. Not only is it hot, but the politics there are killing me."

"I know," Sabrina said again. "Luckily everything is air-conditioned there. And you can give money to the businesses you like."

"Yes, I've already found some drag shows I plan to go to."

Her mother would likely show up in jeans and a blazer wearing comfortable support sandals, instead of the clubbing clothes others would wear. But she'd be first to hoot and holler and would tip with fives and tens instead of the dollars expected.

Sabrina snorted at the vision, her tears starting to slow.

"But I was thinking of spending a few days on Marco Island, between business meetings, if you wanted to join me. We could strategize next steps for your career and catch up."

Sabrina was taken aback. Her mother never went on vacation and never invited her to join her.

"You know," Jacqueline continued. "Just some girl time. We haven't caught up in years. We've both been so busy with our companies. And before you start your next job, I thought . . . . Not a big deal either way if you're busy."

"Let me think about it, mom. I've definitely got some prospects," she lied, so her mom wouldn't feel like Sabrina didn't want to go. And it wasn't that she didn't want to . . . it was just she hadn't taken a vacation with her mother since she was a little girl. What would they do? What would they talk about? What would her mother be like after a few drinks on the beach?

Sabrina's phone buzzed—a new text message. It could wait; it was likely an ad for business clothes she didn't need.

"Oh, that's wonderful news," Jacqueline said. What kind of company? Will you be C-level again or will you need to take a step back? Sometimes that's not a bad thing. You get to know the company without all that executive pressure."

"It's with another marketing company and similar to what I was doing before. Strategy and vision and that type of thing." Sabrina winced, hating lying to her mother, but not sure how to get out of the conversation.

"That makes me feel so much better," Jacqueline said. She

let out a breath, audible across the phone. "I knew you'd be ok. I just... between the divorce and the... restructuring of Thinkfling, I was worried about you."

"Nothing to worry about, mom. I'm fine." The tears welled up again, brought on by the lie. She was not fine.

"Then don't worry about joining me. I know how hard it is to take time off when you start a new job. You have to accrue your PTO and even then, you can't take a day off your first year. You'll lose too much momentum."

"No, I—" Sabrina felt bad. She hadn't decided not to join her mother for the vacation. She'd just wanted a way out in case she needed it. "You never know about these things. Or maybe I could change my start date for after the vacation." God, had she just offered to change her start date for a nonexistent job? She should become a politician with all the lying she was doing lately.

"I have to go," her mother said. "A phone call just came in."

It was ten p.m. on the east coast. There was no way she'd just gotten a call, and her mother was the CEO. She could ignore it. Her mother wanted to get off the phone with HER.

"Go get your call," Sabrina said trying to hide her hurt, though the tears were flowing and dripping down her chin onto her shirt. "I'll let you know about Marco Island. Send me the dates."

"I'm sure your job will come through," her mother said. "You're pretty extraordinary."

The call disconnected and Sabrina wept. She wept in confusion for why her mother had invited her for vacation. She wept in appreciation for the flowers. She wept for the loss of her job and her marriage. She wept for the loss of who she might have been if she'd made different decisions. She wept because it was hard to change. And she wept because she'd messed things up with Johnny, and she'd liked him.

Damnit.

After a few minutes, she pulled herself together, blew her nose, and washed her face. She stared at her reflection, noting the beginnings of wrinkles and sagging skin before turning away. She picked up her phone and glanced down, remembering the text message that had come through.

Her heart plummeted into her stomach.

seventeen

OH-MY-GOD.

Sabrina's phone had sent the rest of the text she'd partially deleted earlier in the day. How had that happened? She pressed on the *Soooooo....* text she'd somehow sent, trying to figure out at what time her phone had betrayed her.

Seventeen minutes ago. She must have somehow hit it when talking to her mom. And now Johnny had responded, thinking she'd intentionally sent the text.

God, this was a nightmare!

She should've deleted Johnny's contact information when she'd decided not to see him again, rather than constantly checking to see if she'd missed a message from him. She should've fully deleted the message she'd decided not to send, so it wouldn't accidentally get sent by the asshole universe.

She knew better. Especially with how the universe was messing with her.

But the text had been sent—somehow—and now Johnny was asking for advice on how to go with the flow? From her? Her life was a mess. Her mother had just lied to get off the phone with her. Before that phone call, she'd spent the last hour reading various reviews on shopping sites so she could choose a new pair of sneakers for the bakery. She'd wanted shoes that were comfy, she could stand in for hours, and were washable in case she spilled anything on them. And without the disposable income she'd once enjoyed as a VP at Thinkfling, she wanted to make a good choice and not waste her money. And she hadn't even purchased anything yet!

An hour of her life gone choosing sneakers. She was taking controlling what she could control to an obsessive level.

And hadn't Johnny been the go-with-the-flow person? The surfer dude who owned his own surfing business? The guy who had taken her to the movies and a random Italian restaurant with no planning or forethought?

He wanted advice from her?

> Her phone buzzed again. It's ok if you're not interested in another date. I'm just feeling confused with some personal stuff I'm dealing with right now. I could use some advice and thought you might be able to help.

If the universe hadn't wanted Johnny in her life again, she would've never seen him at the Boundaries speakeasy and her phone would've never sent that text.

The universe was an asshole but maybe it was trying to help. This was too many coincidences to ignore.

And she liked Johnny.

Sabrina got up, poured a glass of the Tempranillo from the Italian place, and leaned on the Corian counter in her kitchen to type.

> What's going on?

Her phone buzzed immediately.

> I like what I do. But lately, the bureaucracy is getting to me. I think I'm doing more harm than good. I don't know anymore.

> Owning your own business is hard. There's lots of regulations in California. But it's kind of hard to run a surf shop in Colorado.

> True.

She waited to see if he'd say anything else, but the dots didn't start up again. She sipped her wine and thought. She'd actually counseled people on the soul-sucking part of bureaucracy at Thinkfling. The marketing firm was super competitive and super bureaucratic. Johnny wasn't the first person to get caught up in the rules and regulations and forget why he got into owning a surf shop. But she'd always talked people into staying at Thinkfling, or if they weren't useful anymore, or their position and work truly was meaningless—moving on.

She couldn't answer this like bad-ass business bitch Sabrina. She needed to answer it like Breena would. Swallowing another sip of wine, she thought for a minute before texting,

> Do you still find purpose in your business?

The three dots went on for a while before he responded. Sabrina turned on some Brandi Carlile and went back to the couch.

I do. Or I did. I used to think I made a difference, but then something happened. I feel responsible, though I know I'm not. At least not completely.

Oh no. Had someone been injured during a surf lesson? Maybe the board had knocked them unconscious, and they'd drowned. Could that happen? She knew nothing about surfing.

What happened?

I don't want to get into it. But I feel responsible.

She nodded to herself before typing, *People make more of a difference than they think they do. I can see surfing being very empowering and that ripples out into people's lives. But your question was more about the universe and controlling what you can control, right?*

The dots went on for a while, then disappeared. Sabrina picked up an Oprah's Book Club book with a sigh. Maybe Johnny was regretting talking to her, or she hadn't been free-spirited enough for him.

Her phone buzzed. *I'm feeling like maybe I should be doing something else. I mean, I can do other things and inspire others, make change, right?*

You can. What would you do?

Eat at that Italian restaurant.

She pulled the blanket she'd just bought over her legs and sent some laughing emojis.

He responded with a skull.

She added some question marks.

The skull means laughing to death. Teenagers use it. They're too cool for the laughing emojis. That's what us old people use.

Could he have teenage kids? She'd thought he was in his mid-thirties and while old enough to have teenagers, technically, he hadn't seemed like a dad. Maybe he had nieces or nephews. Or just hung out with teenagers in his surf shop. With a shake of her head, she went back to the original question.

Could you be a chef?

I just like to eat. Wish I could get paid for that.

Sabrina giggled again, but before she could respond, Johnny sent another text, *Actually, I'd like to learn how to meditate. Could you show me?*

Her heart dropped. She had no idea how to meditate. She

sucked at it. The last time she'd tried to meditate during yoga she'd run through her shopping list.

But Breena would know how to do it. She could probably meditate in her sleep. Breena's chakras were probably totally in balance, and Sabrina didn't even know what the colors stood for. But Johnny didn't need to know that. *Of course I can show you. There's lots of apps you can try too.* Maybe she could just point him in that direction. Tell him meditation was super personal and everyone did it differently. That there was no "right" way to meditate. Then maybe he wouldn't realize Sabrina sucked at it.

Thank you. But I have another question for you, Johnny texted.

Oh god.

What would you do, if you could do anything?

Phew. *Anything?*

Anything. Bucket list stuff.

She thought about all the stuff she'd always wanted to do but had never tried. Things she'd never even told Nixi or Leroy about. Images of hot air ballooning, writing a book, and snorkeling the Great Barrier Reef flashed through her brain. But there was one thing she wanted. And Breena would want it, too. *I've always wanted a tattoo.*

You don't have one?

I know. Everyone in California does. Do you?

I have a small one on my chest; a Star Wars one.

Oh?

The dots were there for a while before a picture appeared. Johnny showing off an odd circular chest tattoo and some amazing muscles.

How is that Star Wars?

It's the rebel alliance sign.

Sabrina blew up the picture to see what was behind Johnny. She desperately wanted to know more about this man. She could see a bit of a blue couch and a bookshelf stacked high with books. There was no obvious trash or dirt. She spotted a dog bed and a black dog's leg and tail.

Without thinking, she texted, *I see Lando.*

Another picture pinged in, a large black lab, his snout gray.

What a cutie. How old is he?

About seven. He has premature gray.

She giggled again. God, this was the best part of dating; getting to know someone a little piece at a time. She'd missed this. *I like your tattoo.* She winced, hoping he'd see it as flirting and not some creepy response.

Thank you. It's silly, but important to me. What kind of tattoo do you want?

Not sure. Where'd you get yours? I know the artist matters.

Depends on what you want to get. Each artist has their own style, though I'm not an expert. What are you thinking?

What did she want? She didn't know; she'd barely thought about it.

Close your eyes, Johnny texted. *And don't think. Just go with the first thing that pops into your head.*

A jellyfish, she responded.

The three dots were there for a while. *I figured you'd go for the yoga breath one. Why a jellyfish?*

What yoga breath tattoo? She Googled it quickly to find a twisty line tattoo adorning wrists, ankles, and backs. Breena would know what that meant. She'd have to ask her instructor how that line was like a breath before she ran into Johnny again. She went back to her text.

I used to watch for jellyfish when I was a little girl at the beach. Saw a bunch of them, moon jellies, one summer when my mom and I went to Monterey. I like that jellyfish just go wherever the waves take them. Everything is out of their control and yet they thrive. Seems like a good reminder.

Sounds perfect for you.

No, it didn't. It sounded perfect for Breena. Not bad-ass business bitch Sabrina. But she still wanted it.

Where would you get it? Johnny asked.

Sabrina looked down at her body, imagining putting a tattoo on her foot, ankle or back. That's where Breena would get it. But none of those places sounded right, not for her.

I think I'll get it on my wrist.

I'll take you if you want. It helps if you have someone to go with you. Less likely to chicken out.

She drained what was left of her wine, and responded, *I'd like that.*

Me too. This weekend? Don't want you to change your mind.

She took a deep breath, wished for more wine, and began to type.

eighteen

"YOU CALLED me yesterday and told me you had the ingredients for the hot cross buns." Matt folded his arms against his chest. "And I would get them right out of the oven. Still warm. Those are the words you used."

"I know we did," Sabrina said, trying to sound soothing, though she wanted to bang her head on the glass case. "I was the one who called you. We'd made the dough, and it just had to rise overnight. But we couldn't get the oven to work this morning."

A clang sounded from the kitchen where Hattie was trying to fix the broken oven. The lights flickered in Sugar Bliss, and Sabrina winced, hoping Hattie wouldn't blow a fuse and take out all of Encinitas. Instead of calling an electrician, like Sabrina had suggested, Hattie had pulled a beat-up toolbox out of her office and said she knew what the problem was. She'd fix it on her own. "No need for an expensive electrician," had been her exact words.

The lights flickered again, and Hattie let out a muffled yell. Sabrina hoped the owner hadn't electrocuted herself.

LYING, BAKING, & SURFING

"I'm so sorry," she told Matt. "We had the best of intentions and did plan to have the hot cross buns for you."

The older gentleman chewed on his mustache and stared into the empty glass case, like if he looked hard enough, he could conjure up the buns. "So, you have nothing? Not even day olds?"

Sabrina shook her head. "We give them all to the homeless shelter at the end of every day. Hattie has really strict standards about the quality of the goods she sells. She won't sell the day olds."

They hadn't even opened Sugar Bliss this morning, putting a closed sign on the door. Of course, it hadn't stopped the people who had come in yesterday for the coffee cake from trying to come back. The broken oven had come at the worst time!

The air was full of the smell of dough and yeast, as their baked goods overrose. All of their hard work yesterday and this morning, mixing the ingredients, kneading the dough, and building the hot cross buns, croissants, breads, and cinnamon rolls, would get thrown away.

"Hattie's hot cross buns are the best around," Matt muttered. "I just need a win."

"Matt?" Sabrina asked, noting the strain around his lips and the bags under his eyes. "Are you ok?"

"It's not a big deal," he said. "I just . . . it's hard . . . the buns are my daughter's favorite. Please call me again when you actually have them." He turned to go.

"Wait, if you—"

"Oh," he said turning around. "I heard what Thinkfling did to you. It's not fair. That company is crap, and Thomas is an asshole. But it's getting taken care of. You won't have to be here much longer."

"Matt, what are you—?"

"Fucking-A!" Hattie screamed from the back as something else metal jangled to the floor.

"You ok in there?" Sabrina hurried into the kitchen, Matt and his cryptic words forgotten.

Hattie pushed herself back from the oven. "I jammed my finger," she said. "Hurts, but nothing major."

"Is it bleeding?" Sabrina asked, going for the first aid kit.

"Just bruised," Hattie muttered.

"Well, be careful," Sabrina said. "If you hurt yourself, I can't run Sugar Bliss by myself."

"Yeah," Hattie muttered. She sat down in a broken-backed chair, her hands between her legs, and looked around the kitchen—at the giant island they used for kneading and mixing, the industrial mixer, the huge oven, the cooling racks, and all the ingredients and supplies organized on wire shelves around the room.

"Go home," Hattie said, her tone flat. "We won't be selling anything right now if the oven won't heat. I'm sure it's the ignitor because the oven turns on, but I can't figure out how to fix it. Just make sure you lock the door on your way out. I'm going to keep working on it."

"Can I at least look for an electrician?" Sabrina asked. "Just a Google search. They may not come today, but we could get one out here in a day or two so you can reopen."

"Electricians cost too much," Hattie muttered, running her fingers through her graying hair. "This has happened before. I can fix it. It's just . . . this is a lot of ingredients we're losing."

"Hattie, if you really don't have the money, maybe I can help. My savings—"

"Absolutely not," Hattie snapped. "You work for me. I'm not accepting handouts from my employees."

Sabrina understood. If she'd been struggling and one of her employees had offered her money, she'd be offended, too.

"You're right. I'm sorry."

"Just go home," Hattie said. "I'll call you if I get the oven fixed. For now, you get free time. But I can't pay you," she said softly. "If you're not working."

"I know," Sabrina said. "I wouldn't expect it."

Hattie didn't respond, just stared at the floor.

Sabrina untied her apron and tossed it into the dirty linen container. "Will you be, ok?" she asked, her voice gentle.

"Of course," Hattie said. "I've been through worse." To Sabrina though, it looked like the older woman was doing everything she could not to burst into tears.

"Can I get you lunch at least?" Sabrina asked. "Maybe some soup from that place down the street or—"

"Just go. I got this."

Sabrina went, ducking through the front door and trying to figure out how she could help the bakery owner. What would she have done in the past?

The answer came easily, too easily. And she didn't like it. She got into her car, her heart sinking. If she'd still been at Thinkfling, she would've felt a little pity for Hattie and Sugar Bliss for a few minutes, but that would be the end of it. Businesses come and go, and some businesses outlive their usefulness and should close, should get out of the way of newer businesses. Especially a business like Hattie's that was a labor of love and not a true business. She doubted Hattie had a business plan, a budget, or standard operating procedures. In the past, she would've said it was good for Sugar Bliss to close and get out of the way of a business that would be better run and more profitable.

But Hattie didn't seem to have anything else other than the bakery. She didn't talk about a partner or any kids. She didn't even mention any hobbies or anything she did after work. There was no talk of movies, of Netflix series, of books, or even spending a sunny afternoon at Balboa Park. Sabrina had the feeling Hattie went home and tried new recipes to introduce to her bakery. The woman literally had nothing else.

God, what should Sabrina do? What was inside her control? She could give Hattie money, but that didn't feel right, and Hattie didn't want it anyways. She closed her eyes and took a few deep breaths, hoping for intuition or the universe to tell her what to do. But no prophetic song shuffled through her Spotify, a random text message didn't appear, and oddly enough, no sky writers drew a message above her car.

The universe was being silent and unhelpful and all she could do was respect Hattie's wishes and leave. She put the car in gear and headed west, toward the ocean. She told herself she was just driving in a random direction, but in truth, was driving toward Moonlight Beach. Reaching the parking lot she'd locked her car in, she parked and walked down the steps to the sand. The ocean was a smooth blue, and she felt a combination of loss and relief not to see any surfers out.

Whelp, it was a long shot. She wanted to text Johnny, figure out what he was doing, maybe run into him at "random." But that would come off as desperate. Even she knew that. Instead, she texted Nixi.

> Hey. I got a question for you.

> I adore you. You're the best distraction ever. How did you work for this asshole for so long?

> Thomas? There's a reason he goes through so many assistants. The male ones do better. I don't think he likes women.

> Yeah. I've noticed. And since I have no kids—his words, not mine—I can stay late as he needs me to.

LYING, BAKING, & SURFING

> Sounds like you need to quit. Find a bakery where you can knead dough.

> Yeah, I'm already looking. Though no bakeries for me. I'd probably burn whatever I was making. Crank the oven up to 500 to get the cinnamon rolls done faster.

Sabrina shuddered. She knew Nixi wasn't lying. Her former assistant tried to get everything done as fast as possible.

> What'd you need?

> Hattie's oven went out and I don't think she has the money to fix it.

> So, offer to pay for it.

Sabrina tugged her wind-blown hair from her eyes.

> I did. She got mad and told me to leave.

> Fired twice in a month. High five!

> Oh jeez. I don't think she fired me.

If she was fired, it was because Hattie didn't have work for her, not like how Thomas had fired her.

> I think she's just out of money. Got any ideas how to fix that?

> Loan?

> Figure she would've done that if she could. Maybe her credit score is crap.

> GoFundMe? People really liked her apple coffee cake—which was amazing, BTW. I think I gained five pounds off that alone.

> She's an amazing baker. But negative to the GoFundMe. No one contributes to those. Though . . .

An idea occurred to Sabrina.

> Yesterday I posted all over social media. Everyone said they'd forgotten about Sugar Bliss. Then this morning, there were so many people, the same people, trying to come in. Trying to see if we had more coffee cake or another goodie. What about a neighborhood ask? Like a Patreon?

> Hmmmmmm.

The three dots went on for a while Sabrina breathed in the cool breeze off the water, enjoying the view of the ocean. She'd lived close to the beach for so long but had been terrible about taking the time to appreciate it.

> People will want something and if Hattie's that broke, she won't have much to give. And giving people gift cards for the future doesn't work if the business doesn't stay open.

> No, that just puts her further in the hole.

Sabrina kicked off her shoes and started walking across the sand, her feet in the cool surf, dodging seaweed and the big holes children always dug in the sand.

> Whatever we do, I'd have to talk her into it.

> Then it's her choice. I think it's easier if you just loan her the money to fix the oven.

> Good point. That thing is so old, she probably needs another one.

Sabrina's phone rang—Hattie's number. This couldn't be good. "Hello. You ok, Hattie?"

"You need to come back," Hattie said, her voice shaking. "Matt was in an accident."

nineteen

SABRINA JUMPED BACK into her car, heading back toward Sugar Bliss. What on earth had happened to Matt? What kind of accident? Had he fallen? Had he gone back into the bakery?

Where are you? she texted Hattie at a stoplight.

No answer.

She drummed on her steering wheel, waiting for the light change, hoping for a response. Nothing. The light turned green, but only allowed three cars through before turning yellow.

"Son of a bitch! Who designed the timing of these lights?" she asked no one. She imagined some bored guy in front of a computer screen, cackling madly while he watched traffic pile up.

Sabrina shook the image away, turned down her music, and opened her window to listen for sirens. She couldn't hear anything other than traffic and the wind blowing through the palm trees.

Finally, the light changed, and she turned left toward Sugar Bliss. There was an ambulance and firetruck in the intersection close to the shop. Sabrina hit her brakes. Was it for Matt?

Pulling to the shoulder, she jumped from her car and ran up the sidewalk toward the accident. She called Hattie's phone, but there was no answer.

"Damnit," Sabrina muttered, stuffing her phone back into a pocket. She craned her neck, trying to find Hattie or Matt.

The accident looked bad. A black BMW sat in the intersection, a gray Honda next to it. It looked like the BMW had run the red light, slamming into the rear door on the driver's side. Both cars were likely totaled; debris and various liquids staining the street. Onlookers standing on the sidewalk watched the paramedics, hands over their mouths, while traffic control detoured cars around the accident. A middle-aged woman wearing heels and a pencil skirt stood next to the Honda, her phone to her ear. EMTs finished loading a gurney onto an ambulance and slammed the door before Sabrina could see who was on it.

"Hattie?" Sabrina yelled again, finally spotting the older woman sitting on the curb, her hands clasped in her lap. She dropped to her knees beside the woman. "Hattie? What happened?"

The baker looked over at Sabrina, and this time, burst into tears. Sabrina put an arm around her and let her cry, wishing she'd grabbed her purse and could offer a tissue. Luckily, one of the police officers, a tall man with Hispanic features and dark glasses shading his eyes, came over and handed a packet to Hattie.

"I know you're probably all shaken, but can I ask you a few questions?" the man asked. "And then I'll get you on your way."

Hattie nodded, dried her eyes, raised her chin, and took a deep breath. Her features settled and her tears dried up instantly. Sabrina envied her control in this moment. She hadn't even seen the accident and her heart was pounding, her hands shaking.

"Did you see what happened?"

Hattie nodded again, a quick bob.

"Can you describe it?"

Hattie opened her mouth, closed it, and swallowed, her eyes again filling with tears. Her control had only been momentary.

"Take your time," Sabrina said, worried about her employer. She wasn't a young woman, and a heart attack would ensure Sugar Bliss's demise.

"I'm ok," Hattie said, wiping her eyes, heaving a giant breath and then another. "I closed my business early because the oven broke. Sabrina works there." The baker pulled away from Sabrina and stood up, so she was more on eye level with the police officer, though he still towered over her. She shaded her eyes from the bright sun. "I was crossing the street, just needed to get some air, and saw Matt's car—the black one—heading toward the intersection. I waved; I felt bad we didn't have his hot cross buns, and as I raised my hand, the gray car turned left, right in front of him. He tried to stop—god, I'm always going to hear those brakes—but just couldn't."

The police officer nodded, jotting down Hattie's statement in a little notebook. "Do you think the black car, Matt, was speeding or anything?"

Hattie shook her head. "There's no way he would. And I never thought, oh look there's Matt, and oh gee golly, he's driving so fast."

Sabrina chortled, and her cheeks flamed red. What was wrong with her?

"It's the adrenaline," the police officer said with a kind look. "It makes your emotions behave unpredictably."

Sabrina nodded, but still felt embarrassed.

He turned back to Hattie. "Do you think he was drinking or under the influence or anything?"

Hattie shook her head again. "He's a pretty boring guy. Just wants to convince his daughter to move in with him, so they're both not so lonely."

"Oh, Hattie," Sabrina said.

"I know you can't tell me; I'm not family," Hattie said to the officer. "But do you think he'll be ok?"

The officer grimaced, his expression hard to read behind the sunglasses.

"They're old friends," Sabrina supplied. "Hattie's store is Sugar Bliss, the bakery. It's been here forever, and Matt is one of her best customers."

"Sugar Bliss," the police officer said. "I used to go there on Sunday mornings when I was a teenager. You had the best cinnamon rolls."

"We still do," Sabrina said. "Baked fresh every day. How about a little info for a baker's dozen?"

She knew Hattie was worried when Hattie didn't react to giving things away; she just leaned in.

"They're transporting the gentleman as a precaution. The seat belt caught him, and he was having chest pain, but pretty sure it was related to the seat belt. You should call him once he's been admitted."

Hattie shook her head. "I don't think I have his number."

"That I can't give you," the officer said. "Even for a hundred cinnamon rolls."

Hattie's lips quirked up slightly and she dried her tears with the tissue. "I know. It's ok. Not sure I could make a hundred, anyway."

"Are you ok to get back to your business?" The officer flipped his sunglasses up onto his forehead and held Sabrina's eyes with his own. She got the message. She needed to keep an eye on Hattie. "Seeing an accident can shake you up."

"I'm fine," Hattie said, raising her chin, her tears once again gone. "I'll just head back to my bakery and keep working on the oven. We won't open tomorrow without it."

"I'll drive you," Sabrina said.

"No, I—"

"It's on my way." Sabrina nodded at the police officer, and he nodded back, relieved someone was taking care of Hattie.

They rode back to Sugar Bliss in silence, and Sabrina pulled up to the closed shop. "I wish we had the hot cross buns for Matt," Hattie murmured. "I could drop them off at the hospital. Try to find his daughter. Maybe find out if he's ok."

"Well, I have an oven at my house," Sabrina said. "And a big counter. Let's take a dozen of the risen hot cross buns back to my place—it's only a few blocks away—and then we can deliver them to the hospital."

Hattie shook her head. "They've over-risen. They won't be as good."

"Hattie, even your over-risen hot cross buns are better than any other bakery's. Let's just grab them. What's the worst that happens?"

Hattie thought for a second and then nodded. "Life's too short," she quipped. "Eat the cake."

"Oh, you're a genius," Sabrina said as they got out of the car and Hattie unlocked the door to Sugar Bliss. "If I was doing your marketing, we'd use that. Except I might change it to, 'eat the hot cross bun.'" She snapped her fingers. "Oh, I got it! 'Life's too short. Buy the hot cross bun!' We could put it on stickers, t-shirts, coffee mugs."

"Maybe if we get the oven fixed, we can do something like that," Hattie said. "But first the oven. Marketing won't do any good if we don't have anything to bake in."

Working quickly, the two women wrapped the trays in plastic wrap and transported them to the backseat of Sabrina's car. Braking and turning carefully, Sabrina drove the few blocks to her house, letting Hattie inside. Within an hour, they'd baked the hot cross buns, and Hattie had taught Sabrina how to make the caramel sauce to drizzle over the top from scratch. Packing a dozen carefully into a box, Sabrina drove Hattie back to Sugar Bliss, where Hattie would take her car and the buns to the hospital.

The sun was setting into the ocean as Sabrina ordered Thai for pickup. Her phone buzzed.

> Still on to get your tattoo tomorrow?

Johnny asked.

> I booked a tattoo artist for a quick sketch. Figured you didn't want anything too crazy.

> I haven't looked at any jellyfish tattoos, she texted back. Today was crazy.

> Me too. TGIF. Just me, the couch, Lando, and a little horror flick, called Shutter for tonight.

Maybe she should seriously consider getting a cat. The idea of sitting on the couch, watching a movie, eating Thai with a critter purring next to her sounded perfect. And something she'd never have taken the time to even consider when she worked at Thinkfling.

> I think I'll copy you. But not the horror movie. Maybe Outlander on Netflix. Supposed to be good.

> Chick-flick. :)

> And that sounds perfect.

She pulled into the restaurant's parking lot.

> So still on for tomorrow for tattoos?

> Don't chicken out. Research tattoos while you're watching blonde-time-traveling Scotsman who says sasquatch with the Scottish accent and makes girls swoon.

> ??

> Sasquatch.

> Sasquatch.

> Fuck.

Sabrina giggled, got out of her car, and collected her takeout.

> Whatever word he uses that all the girls go crazy for. Some Scottish thing.

> Thought Outlander was a chick-flick.

He didn't respond until she pulled into her driveway.

> That's a long story. Tell you while you're getting your tattoo? I scheduled us for eleven tomorrow. Should take a few hours if you need to take time off work. Do you have someone who teaches classes for you? Or do you teach your own yoga classes?

> I have someone

Sabrina envisioned a tall, lithe woman bending herself into various shapes with serenity while others tried to copy her.

LYING, BAKING, & SURFING

> She's really good.

> You'll have to text me her class times.

Sabrina responded with a thumbs up and hoped he wouldn't ask again.

> Do you have someone to cover for you at the shop?

The dots went on for a while. Did he run his surf shop by himself? The single-owner businesses she'd worked with in the past took a level of dedication, intensity, and insanity she just didn't see in Johnny. Maybe he was independently wealthy and while he owned the shop, someone else actually ran it.

> I have a college student. He handles all the board rentals, makes people sign the disclaimers, and return them on time. Sells the snacks and t-shirts and stuff.

She went inside her house, the ghostly smells of the hot cross buns overpowering her curry. Setting the bag on the counter, she looked at her blank forearm. A small tattoo would look good there, right?

What was the worst that could happen?

> I'll see you at 11. Enjoy your movie.

twenty

JONATHAN HELD open the door to High Tide Tattoo for Breena. He'd wanted to pick her up at her place, get a hint of where she lived. He imagined she lived close to the beach, in a funky, older apartment full of mismatched furniture that somehow went together and a balcony full of plants. But she'd refused and requested to be picked up at the same coffee place where they'd had their first date. He tried not to let it bug him.

> Let's keep some things a secret still.

Sabrina had told him via text that morning when he'd requested her address. And while he appreciated her style of dating, he really wanted to know more about her.

And was tired of thinking about work.

The parents had increased their attacks on him after he'd misspoken in a class, making a smart-ass comment that had hurt a student's feelings. Normally he'd have apologized, learned a lesson, and tried to be more careful, but now the parents had added "bully" to their complaints against him. They'd taken his comment out of context and exaggerated it on neighborhood Facebook pages, to the point that any parent or student trying to defend him got virtually shouted down and attacked themselves. He was glad he hadn't given Breena his actual last name so she couldn't track him down and see all this vitriol.

The supportive texts and personal messages from other parents and students had helped a bit. Most remembered him fondly, or at least told him they felt bad for him. His vice principal had advised to keep his head down and offered to let him take a paid leave of absence until things died down. Out of sight, out of mind and all of that. But damn-it—his students needed him. And he wasn't going to let the parents win. He hadn't done anything wrong.

Whatever. He needed to let it go and enjoy being with Breena as she got her first tattoo.

The tattoo artist, a tall woman with white hair and a complex sleeve of tattoos up and down her bare arms turned around as they came into the shop.

"Breena?" the artist said, holding out her hand. "Estella. I hear you're getting your first tattoo."

"Yes?"

Estella laughed at Breena's questioning tone. "It'll be fine. It's a little one, right?"

"I hope so."

Estella laughed again. "I'll make sure it's small. And do you know what you want?"

"I'd like a jellyfish. On my wrist. And I have some ideas," she said, pulling an iPad out of her hobo bag. "But I'm open to suggestions, or if you don't think something would work. You're the professional."

Jonathan stopped listening to stare at Breena as the two women bent over Breena's iPad. Breena tugged some of her curly hair out of her face and then laughed at something Estella said, throwing her head back and cackling. Jonathan grinned in response, his heart beating faster, though he hadn't listened to the joke. He just loved being with this woman and her laid-back way of looking at things.

"Ok," Estella said. "I think I've got some ideas. Let me draw up a quick sketch. Give me a couple of minutes and then we'll see if that works for you." The artist spun her chair around to a desk, her pencil scratching as she bent over a piece of paper.

Breena moved away to look at the pictures on the walls, while sipping on a giant green smoothie. She winced slightly, swallowing. Must be bitter, but likely very healthy. He admired that she'd do the hard things to stay healthy, whereas he just liked food and wasn't as careful about it being healthy.

She leaned in to inspect a picture and Jonathan joined her. Some of the framed photos were tattoos, but many were seaside locations, old falling-apart buildings in black and white. She pointed one out to him. "I think I know where that is. I used to wo— I know where it is. You can see it from the 101 if you know where to look."

"We should go one day. I love checking out abandoned buildings."

"Really? Why?" She stared up at him, waiting for an answer and he had a sudden inclination. He leaned forward and gave her a gentle kiss. She tasted like a salad—healthy and vibrant.

"What was that for?" she asked.

"Because you really wanted to know. And to answer, I just like them. I think it's the movie guy in me that just likes the what-ifs in an abandoned building. Your turn."

"For a question?" she smiled. "Go for it."

"You sure you want a jellyfish tattoo? Have to ask."

She raised her eyebrows. "I am. Just sounded right. And that's what I'm doing—going with the flow. A jellyfish tattoo sounded right, so I'm getting one."

"Those are the best tattoos," Estella chimed in, still bent over her sketch pad. "The ones that feel right with who you are, right now. I've never understood the 'but-maybe-you'll-change-and-won't-like-it,' reason not to get a tattoo. Of course, we're going to change; that's the point of getting the tattoo. It's a tribute to who we are in the moment." She whipped back around with a drawing of the tattoo for Breena's wrist, a jellyfish with a wide body and subtle trailing tentacles. "Like it? Though I would recommend it go on your forearm instead of your wrist," Estella said, showing Breena how it would flip.

"It's perfect," Breena said. "You drew a purple-striped jellyfish instead of a moon jelly."

"I did," the tattoo artist said with a fist bump for Breena. "Moon jellies have the giant bodies, but you showed me pictures of the purple-striped ones with the long tentacles. I figured this was the best one for you. She looked Breena's leggings, patterned tunic top and green skirt up and down. "It's more elegant, more you."

"So, how do you know about jellyfish?" Jonathan asked as Breena got settled in the chair, her arm prepped and was cautioned not to move. Estella dipped her tattoo pen into the ink and began to draw.

Breena winced at the sting, but answered, "Googled a bunch of jellyfish pictures last night. The names just stuck with me. You ever been stung by one when you're surfing?"

"Thank god, no. But I stepped on a stingray once. Couldn't stand in my classroom for a week."

"Classroom?"

Jonathan's stomach lurched. He should just come clean and tell her he was a history teacher, not an owner of a surf shop. A terrible teacher about to get fired if the parents won.

"Well, my classroom—" He couldn't do it. He couldn't admit he'd been lying all this time. "That's what I call the back room in my shop where I go over the dos and don'ts of surfing. It's nice to be out of the way of all the people shopping." God, he was an idiot. She would find out the truth eventually.

"Once this is healed, you'll have to take me out surfing," Breena said. Her phone in her purse vibrated, and she glanced at her hobo bag.

"Don't move," Estella said.

"No worries," Breena said. "Can't be that important." She winced again as Estella bent over her arm, the tattoo pen buzzing.

"You ok?" Estella asked. "This one won't take long. It's the multi-hour ones that really get to people."

"Yeah, it just feels weird. Hurts a bit, but it's more annoying than anything."

"Your nerves go dead pretty quick. Just try not to move."

Breena's purse vibrated again. And again, and again.

"Godd—darn-dang it," Breena said at the fifth buzz, sounding like one of his students trying not to curse in front of the teacher. "I hope nothing's wrong. Hey Johnny, can you just check my phone for me?"

"You sure?"

She smiled. "My life is an open book."

Johnny opened her purse, surprised at how organized it was. Everything was compartmentalized into smaller bags of medicine, a sewing kit, and tampons, her wallet and phone. He pulled it out and held it up to Breena's face to unlock the screen. "Looks like someone named Nixi was texting." He scanned the text. "Something about Thomas being an asshole and that it's confirmed they lost the Barajas account. Guess Thomas is on the war path, and someone suggested they call you?" He kept scrolling as more texts kept coming in. "Sounds pretty intense. Do you want me to hold the phone up to your ear so you can talk?"

"We can take a break if you need to," Estella said.

"It's nothing big," Breena said, though her tight lips and red cheeks said otherwise. "You can put my phone back into my purse. I'll text her once we're done."

Johnny shrugged and went to put her phone back, but it buzzed again. "Now it's a Hattie," he told her.

"Oh? Does she say anything about a Matt?"

"She says she dropped the buns off at the hospital yesterday, but couldn't get in to see Matt," Jonathan read off the screen.

Breena nodded. "Does it say if Matt's ok?"

"Do you want me to type that?"

"Yes, please."

He asked the question. And read back the quick response. "Nothing. I think he's still in the hospital, and I'm not going to wait in the lobby like a stalker for his daughter."

"Makes sense," Breena said. "Can you tell Hattie that I'll keep thinking good thoughts and I hope we see him soon?"

He typed out the message and received a thumbs up in response.

"Who's Matt?" he asked.

"Oh, my . . . friend Hattie saw her friend Matt get into a car accident yesterday. Someone turned left in front of him, and he hit the other car. And then he got taken to the hospital with chest pain. She took him a gift, but since she's not family, the nurses won't tell her how he's doing."

It reminded him of Lily. He'd known something was wrong when she hadn't shown up for class to take her finals. She'd been nervous about the test and her parents' reaction if she'd failed, but he'd figured they would've forced her to go to school. In the afternoon, Luz had told him the teenager had been hospitalized and then nothing more, and he'd felt the same sense of helpless concern; wanting to know more but trying to respect the family boundaries.

He never would've dreamed Lily would've taken every pill in the medicine cabinet because dying was easier than failing her finals.

"You ok?" Breena asked, her eyes on his. "You went away there for a minute. Do you need to sit down?"

"I'm ok," he said. "I just . . . why do bad things happen?"

"I don't know," Breena said, fully focused on him, despite the tattoo pen buzzing in the background. It made him feel as if he was the only person in her world. "There's a ton of bull about how you have to go through the bad stuff to get to the good stuff or how life is cyclical. Or to choose happiness no matter what's going on in life. Just find the happy stuff."

"Tell that to the homeless people out on the street," Estella chimed in. "Just think happy thoughts and you'll be fine."

"Yeah, it's ridiculous," Breena said, raising her eyebrows. "I wish I knew why bad things happened. I wish I could stop them."

"We all do," Jonathan said.

The room fell into silence for a few minutes, broken only by the buzzing of Estella's tattoo pen.

"And done," Estella said, leaning back. Breena inspected the tattoo while the other woman wiped away excess blood and ink.

"It's perfect," Breena said.

And it was. The jellyfish was flatter than he would've expected, but with long curling tentacles thicker by the body. It wasn't cartoon like, like some tattoos were, but elegant and spontaneous.

Breena waggled her eyebrows at him. "You going to get one?"

Estella leaned back. "I have time for a small one. My next client isn't until two."

Jonathan looked into Breena's laughing eyes. God, she was incredible. "Sure."

Breena vacated the chair. "Whatcha going to get?"

"You get to pick."

"Anything I want?"

"Anything. Whatever you think I would like. Whatever speaks to you about letting go of things I can't control. Cuz I gotta get better about that."

"Hmmmmm... I have an idea."

twenty-one

SABRINA INSPECTED her plastic wrapped forearm. The tattoo burned and itched a bit, but not unmanageably. The subtle purple, yellow, and turquoise colors of her jellyfish tattoo stared back at her, slightly distorted through the plastic. She leaned across the table, touching Johnny's hand, and managing not to knock over her cocktail glass.

"Let me see yours again."

He rolled up the sleeve on his black t-shirt and she inspected the tattoo she'd chosen for him; an edgy black and gray wave Estella had gone overboard sketching. Sabrina had known she'd chosen the right tattoo for Johnny when his blue-green eyes had lit up when Estella presented it to him.

Now they were celebrating with a late lunch (another salad without meat for Sabrina—yay) at a Tiki-themed restaurant in downtown Carlsbad. It had every cliché—from bamboo chairs and tables, to fake plants dangling from the ceiling, and fake parrots staring down at patrons from the bar shelves. While the food was decent, locals and tourists really came for the rum drinks, served in giant tiki mugs, the alcohol sometimes set ablaze.

Sabrina sipped her cocktail, a juice and rum concoction she drank through a straw in a tiki mug shaped like a pirate ship with a scantily clad mermaid on the bow. She'd only had one drink; but already felt buzzed—maybe it was the adrenaline from the tattoo. Or maybe it was from just doing things without decision or thought.

And now she had a tattoo! And a really cool one she adored.

Sabrina's eyes fell on a couple being led to a corner booth. Oh, that was interesting. Her last text from Nixi had been:

> That's it. I'm done for the day. I got plans.

She'd responded with:

> let me know if you want to talk. Sorry about the Barajas account.

Guess she now knew what Nixi's plans had been.

"Hey, hey," she told Johnny, jerking her chin toward the couple.

He turned around.

"No, no, don't look," Sabrina said.

He grinned. "What would you like me to do?"

"It's Nixi and Kaito," she said with a laugh. "They must be on a date or something. Did you know they'd started seeing each other?"

Johnny spun around. "That liar told me he couldn't go surfing today because he had to grade papers. Guess he just had a hot date."

"Yeah, Nixi didn't tell me either." She picked up her phone, planning to text her friend, but then Nixi let out a peal of laughter as the couple sat. They seemed to be having a great time and Sabrina decided not to ruin it. Nixi probably needed to blow off some steam anyways.

"I wonder if they're going to notice us," Johnny said. "Maybe we'll say something when we leave."

Their server came over and asked if they wanted another round just as a different server delivered a giant drink in a green robot tiki to Nixi and Kaito's table. It had two twisty straws sticking out of the top.

"We'll have one of those," Sabrina said, pointing at the robot tiki mug.

The server nodded and walked away. Johnny turned to look at the drink and raised his eyebrow. "That looks intense."

"Oh!" Sabrina said, her cheeks flushing. "I didn't even ask if you had any other plans for the day. I'm sorry. I can cancel it."

"I'm not doing anything," Johnny said. "The day is yours." He took her hand and raised it to his lips, his eyes flirting with hers. Daring, she leaned over the table and kissed him, her blood thrumming with desire. Maybe the universe wasn't the asshole she'd thought.

"Thank you for the tattoo," she said. "And booking it and going with me. This is much bigger than just getting a tattoo for me."

He smiled and dragged a fry through ketchup. "So other than yoga and watching sexy Scotsmen, what do you like to do?"

Sabrina thought before answering. The lie about owning a yoga studio was beginning to grate on her. There'd already been a few uncomfortable moments when he'd asked her questions she had to lie about. He wasn't even using her real name and at some point, he'd want to stop by her yoga studio or learn about meditation from her, which she still sucked at. But she wasn't ready to confess she worked at a bakery or was a fired C-level executive either. And other than doing yoga, reading, and watching Netflix occasionally, what else did she do? Maybe she could tell him the truth gradually?

"I actually like baking," she answered finally. "There's just something about kneading dough and watching it rise and then putting it in the oven."

"What do you like to make?"

"Hot cross buns, sticky buns. That type of thing. Bread is actually really satisfying to make and it's not as sweet. I'll bring you some."

"Thanks. I can bring it to my—coworkers."

"The college kid that watches your store?" she asked, taking a sip of the drink, and wincing a bit at the overly sweet flavor of pineapple, orange, guava, and rum.

"Exactly," he said, talking faster. "These college kids have it rough; they're all surviving on ramen and have a billion roommates. He'll love it."

"Your turn!" she said a bit loudly, the alcohol loosening her up a bit too much. What do you do for fun other than watching horror movies and surfing and selling surf boards? Oh!" She pulled out her phone. "I want to book a surf lesson. But I want it to go through your store and everything. No deals and I want the same lessons in your classroom everyone else gets. I know how hard it is to run a business and every penny counts."

"We'll look at the calendar later," he said. "The booking app was being . . . wonky this morning. We were taking sign-ups on paper, and it's been a mess."

"Your college student must be good," she said. "He hasn't called you once."

"He is. I wish I could pay him more." He looked down at his plate, but his fries were gone. For a second Sabrina had the odd idea he was contemplating licking the ketchup from the plate. Instead, he shifted in his chair like he couldn't get comfortable.

"So what do I do for fun?" Johnny asked. "I take Lando for walks, surf with friends. I like all the San Diego clichés—fish tacos and going to see the Padres and drinking IPAs from craft breweries."

"Did you figure out what you wanted to do about your business? Whether you still want to keep doing it? Whether it still brings you joy?"

He rubbed the spot between his eyes. "No," he said shortly. "Things are getting worse. And I don't think I want to talk about it today."

Whoops. Guess she shouldn't have asked for surf lessons.

He took a big slurp of the drink, not looking at her.

"Totally get it," she said. "Let's have fun today. What should we do next?"

Before he could answer, Nixi slid into the booth next to her, tossing her braided hair over a shoulder. "We saw you. Thought we'd join you."

Kaito put their giant drink on the table and sat next to Johnny.

"What are you two up to?" Nixi asked.

"We got tattoos," Sabrina said, showing Nixi her arm.

"You got a tattoo! You?" Nixi inspected the jellyfish. "It's really good." She turned to Johnny. "Did you get one too?"

"She talked me into it," Johnny said, rolling up his sleeve.

"Nice," Kaito responded while Nixi gave it a thumbs up.

"What are you guys doing?" Johnny asked.

"A few drinks, dinner, and then we'll head to the Belly Up for a show," Nixi said. "You guys want to join? I think there's still tickets."

"Who's—" Sabrina stopped herself. Who was playing was outside her control. She wanted to go, wanted to have fun with friends and the band didn't matter. "Want to go?" she asked Johnny.

"Why not?"

"Oh, but before we go, I need to talk to Sabrina," Nixi said. She took Sabrina's hand and pulled her out of the booth, leading her to the sidewalk outside. Tourists in sundresses, hoodies, and shorts passed them, shopping in the funky beachy stores and stopping for snacks from a food truck set up in the parking lot.

"I saw all your texts." Sabrina said, tugging her hair out of her eyes. "Sorry I didn't respond when you were sending them."

"Oh, you were busy," Nixi said with a wave of her arm. "Not a big deal. But I want to—"

"I know I shouldn't care about the Barajas account, but I worked so hard on that. And they were such a nice family."

"Yeah, but because we lost that account, Thomas resigned." Nixi flipped her hair.

"And the word is the board asked for his resignation. And the Barajas account was just the tip of the iceberg. He did something . . . but none of us know what."

"I think I do," Sabrina said, her stomach dropping and the alcohol swirling. "Or I suspect. Just instinct; he was a little too close to some of the staff, if you know what I mean."

"You didn't say anything about that."

"I knew nothing. It was—" Sabrina thought back and tried to explain. "Expressions as text messages came in. How he looked at people. People leaving his office, that shouldn't be in there. I don't know. It was instinct, but I didn't know anything. And I kept telling myself I was wrong; just misreading the situation." She put her hand over her mouth. "And I didn't like Thomas, so I just thought it was in my head. And it was guys and girls too, so again . . . but that doesn't mean anything."

"It doesn't," Nixi agreed. "Do you think he thought you knew, and that's why he fired you?"

Sabrina grew nauseous. "I don't think so. I made some

mistakes," she said. "I missed some deadlines and one of the directors who reported to me made a bunch of mistakes. Those were all on me. I'm in charge and if my staff are failing, that's on me."

"You're being too hard on yourself. You can't control others. Anyways . . ." Nixi took Sabrina's hand. "Rumor is that you're getting your job back. Actually, the big rumor is that the board is going to ask you to be the next CEO."

Sabrina swayed slightly, and Nixi caught her arm. Thoughts warred against each other. This was her dream, all her plans, all her sacrifices might be worth it. But instead of jubilation, she felt resignation.

"Kind of thought you'd be happier," Nixi said. "We could celebrate today. What's wrong?"

"I don't know if I want to go back," Sabrina whispered, tears springing up in her eyes. "But I don't know who I am without Thinkfling." She stared down at the tattoo on her forearm. If she went with the flow like the jellyfish, she'd flow back to Thinkfling.

"You are Sabrina," Nixi said. "My friend. You're a bad-ass business bitch, but a lot more than that too. And there's a hot guy in there who can't take his eyes off you."

"Kaito likes you too."

"I know," Nixi answered. "So, let's just have fun tonight. Let's go get drunk with those hot guys and see a random band we've never heard of."

Sabrina glanced through the window and saw the two men chatting. Kaito laughed, throwing his head back. She really was starting to like Johnny. Leroy never would've booked her to get a tattoo. And he was so good looking; she'd gotten a good look at his arms when he'd sat for the tattoo. Lust warred with confusion and anxiety.

"Ok," Sabrina said. "Sounds like fun." She wouldn't worry about the future; not tonight. She'd just be. Just exist. Pretend to be a jellyfish and ride the waves to wherever the evening took her.

twenty-two

JOHNNY BROUGHT Sabrina a blueberry sour beer in a giant plastic cup. "Holy cow," she told him as he placed it and his equally large IPA on their table at the Belly Up.

The roadies were working the stage, breaking down the opening band and setting up the instruments for the headliner. Couples and groups mingled in front of the stage, around it, and above. Those with a coveted chair or table didn't move from their places except to send someone to get more drinks. The smell of beer and a bit of pot dominated the room, small puffs of smoke dissipating from the crowd occasionally. An arm waved, beckoning a friend over while someone else laughed. Dimly lit, the entire room hummed with laughter and conversation, while the roadies did a sound check in the background.

"If it's too much, I'll drink the other half of the beer," Johnny said, grabbing the stool next to Sabrina's. "Just drink what you want—places like this only drinks in the giant cups. But I think you'll like this one. Doesn't even taste like a beer."

Obligingly, she took a sip, surprised by the slightly sour, fruity taste. "It's good," she told him and went back to watching the roadies. She knew she should laugh and flirt with him; she enjoyed his company, but right now it felt like too much effort. Despite her desire to let the future go and only focus on tonight, she just couldn't. She didn't know who Breena was, the yoga studio owner who went to UC Davis and had worked at a winery. But she didn't know who Sabrina was either. Nixi's news dominated her thoughts.

The last few weeks as a baker, trying to embrace being a free spirit, had been amusing. It had been fun to pretend to follow the universe's confusing and contradictory guidance, but she was a C-level executive, a bad-ass business bitch through and through. Planning, execution, workflows, meetings with her team, and with her clients were where she shone. She certainly wasn't shining as a baker. A place like Thinkfling was where she belonged, right? Not in this noisy, crowded, slightly smoky room.

She watched a roadie step up to a mic and speak into it, the faint sound echoing a bit, while another taped a sheet of paper, probably the set list, in front of the mic.

Meeting her goals, achieving success and happiness, meant sacrificing everything, everyone around her. It meant giving up on all her other dreams, except to be a CEO. It meant not enough sleep, working late, up early. No lunches, except working lunches, no time to go to the beach, no time to go on a hike, too tired to go to a concert like this.

No time for romance. No time to maintain a marriage or have children.

It meant becoming like her mother, and she admired her mother. Admired all she'd achieved. And Sabrina did love being a bad-ass business bitch. She loved being a C-level executive. She truly found it fun and fulfilling. It just demanded everything she was and there was nothing left over for whoever she might actually be.

Johnny leaned over to whisper in her ear. "You ok? Do you want to go?"

"No, I'm sorry," Sabrina said, pushing away her thoughts. "I'm here."

"Good." He took her hand and kissed it. She leaned forward to kiss him, a gentle kiss, a promise to him and herself to be present. He tasted of beer and a bit of the rum drink they'd shared earlier in the day. She darted her tongue into his mouth, tasting him further. He tasted like the sun, and the surf and mornings lounging in bed, and brunches without plans, and experiences she couldn't fathom.

He let out a small groan when she pulled away. "You're gorgeous," he whispered in her ear, putting his arm around her, his lips against her ear making her skin tingle.

She looked down at her tattoo, staring at the gentle waving tentacles of the jellyfish, and what it meant. Tomorrow would come, the time would pass whether she obsessed over her future or not. And she wanted to be here, with this horror movie-loving surfer.

"I can't wait to watch you do yoga," he whispered in her ear, dousing her libido. Oh yeah, that lie. She drained more of her beer, trying to push away the anxiety. She needed to tell him she wasn't a yoga studio owner at some point.

Right?

Next to her, Nixi chuckled, and Kaito leaned back to sip at his beer. The other couple weren't quite making out, but it was getting close with lots of nuzzles, and hands rubbing thighs and knees beneath the table. Sabrina was betting they wouldn't make it through the headliner's set before grabbing an Uber to one of their homes.

Johnny's hand moved beneath the table, brushing her thigh, a light sensation, testing the waters, seeing what her reaction would be. It was oddly sensual. She focused on the feeling, heat and lust returning to sing through her blood, arcing to her core, making her take a deep breath. She tried to remember if Leroy had ever flirted with her like this, but they'd been so young when they dated. Leroy had been sweet and earnest, but it had taken them time to learn from each other.

But Johnny seemed like he knew what he was doing, brushing her thigh again. He leaned close to whisper in her ear, his lips grazing her neck, his breath hot against her sensitive skin. She suppressed a shiver, more focused on the sensation than what he was saying.

"What?" she said with a smile when he pulled away.

He did it again, leaning in, his lips brushing her ear, his hand gripping her thigh now. She shivered.

"Have you heard of Nebular Dandelions before?"

"Oh, no," she said, her breath coming fast, barely able to focus on finding words. "I haven't."

"They put on a good show," Johnny said as the room darkened, and the crowd cheered. "I've seen the lead singer with other bands; she's fantastic." He pulled her to her feet, her hand enclosed in his. The all-woman band came out, said a few words, and started playing. The crowd moved, cheering, dancing, and singing along.

"Wow," Sabrina half-shouted to Johnny. "I didn't realize how popular they would be."

"They have a huge fan-base here," he said.

The two couples stayed on their feet through the first song, then gradually sat as the music slowed. Nebular Dandelions had a unique blending of bohemian, jazz and folk with a saxophone player, a bongo player, a string quartet and three people on guitars. Sabrina's worries about Thinkfling tried to push through and she closed her eyes, the stage lights shifting in front of her closed lids. She focused on the notes mingling together, the sound of people singing along and chattering, the feel of the music coming through the floor, and the smell of beer and pot. Johnny's hand continued to lightly caress her thigh. She put her hand on his leg and leaned over to kiss him, her tongue darting into his mouth. She was here and nothing was going to ruin that.

* * *

Sabrina had been right; Nixi and Kaito spent much of the show kissing, stroking and being generally obnoxious. As predicted, they'd taken off about halfway through the set, Nixi throwing her arm around Sabrina and whispering, "Go back to Johnny's place with him. It's perfect. And that teacher is going through a really hard time. He needs a distraction."

Teacher?

"Don't think," Nixi whispered, squeezing her arm. "Just follow the universe."

"What if the universe is telling me to go back to Thinkfling?"

"It's not telling you to do that today," she said, climbing off her stool, grabbing Kaito's hand, and heading out the door.

"She ok?" Johnny asked, misinterpreting her expression of worry. "Kaito's a good guy, he won't—"

"Nixi knows what she's doing," Sabrina said. "I'm not worried about her."

"Good." He ran his hand up her arm, leaned over and kissed her, trailing his lips down her neck. She let out a small moan, mostly covered by the applause of the crowd. He pulled away with a grin and stood to cheer for the band.

When the final encore came, she clapped and cheered along with everyone else. In all the noise, Johnny leaned over. "Nightcap at my place?" he asked, his lips sending heat to her center.

She looked up into his eyes, shadowed by the stage lighting. "I'd like that," she said. "I'd like to see where you live and meet Lando."

He took her hand, and following the crowd, went out onto the street. They walked several blocks until their Uber found them. Focusing on not thinking, just reacting, she got into the backseat, pushing aside her rational voice that was demanding to know what she was doing. Johnny put his arm around her and gently nibbled on her neck while the Uber driver pretended to ignore them.

twenty-three

JOHNATHAN UNLOCKED the door to his condo in Carlsbad and let Breena step inside, his hand on the small of her back. He breathed in her scent—cinnamon and vanilla, with a hint of pot still clinging to her clothes from the concert—and tried to forget how the Uber driver had given him the little nod when pulling away; the good-job-bro-nod. It killed his mood a bit, made him feel like a player. He didn't normally bring women back to his condo, and Breena was special. He was hoping tonight would be the first of many nights together, if he was being honest.

"This is nice," Breena said, looking around his condo at the vintage horror movie posters, the bookshelves full of books, and the comfortable, if slightly worn, furniture.

A giant black lab, gray around his muzzle, shuffled to his feet from his bed in front of the television and came over to inspect Breena. This was the ultimate test; how would she respond to Lando? You couldn't fake whether you liked animals, and Lando was a great litmus test. And if Lando didn't like her, then it was game over. No matter how wonderful she was, he'd call this evening to an end and never see her again.

LYING, BAKING, & SURFING

Lando sniffed at Breena's knees, and she held out her hand for him. When he huffed into her hand, giving her his blessing, she patted his head. He looked up at her, his mouth open in a doggy grin.

"Lando," she murmured. "I presume. Your namesake became a general." She smiled up at Jonathan. "I did a Google search. Lando Calrissian is a popular character."

"My older brother used to call him a bad-ass."

"I can see that," Breena said with a chuckle. "Are you a bad-ass?" she asked Lando.

"He's just a goof," Jonathan said. "Who does like getting his ears rubbed."

She moved to scratch the dog behind his ears, and Lando panted with contentment as her fingers found the perfect spot. "I just realized I haven't petted a dog in years. I haven't had one, and I was always too . . . I guess I didn't have any friends with one."

"No siblings with a dog?"

"No siblings," she said. "Just my mom and me. And she was too busy for us to get a dog." Lando let out a lab-sigh of contentment and a faint woof as she dug into the space between his ears and skull.

"What happened to your dad?"

She waggled her eyebrows. "Oh, that's some gossip. I didn't have one. My mom went to a sperm bank, or so she says. With an adult lens on things she'd said when I was little, I think her heart was broken before I was born, but she decided she wanted a baby, without dealing with a husband or a partner. As far as I know, she's never dated after I was born."

"Even today?"

Breena shook her head. "She works too much and says dating is too much effort. She's too set in her ways and what would she want a guy for anyways?"

Lando shuffled so he could lie on his back, exposing his belly for belly rubs. She kneeled next to the dog, her green skirt pooling around her, obliging him while the lab grinned at her.

Perfect.

"What would you like to drink?" Jonathan asked, heading into the kitchen. "I have wine, beer, water."

"Wine is perfect," she said, her smile audible in her voice. Lando let out a grumbling woof, and she laughed, a deep belly-laugh.

Johnathan stuck his head into the living room, a corkscrew in one hand. Breena was still rubbing Lando's belly but now with both hands, while Lando's tongue rolled in ecstasy. He met Jonathan's eyes, seeming to say, "don't let this woman go."

He didn't intend to. He handed Breena her wine, and she stood, shaking fur from her hands, and moving to inspect his bookshelves. She ran her fingers over the book spines—obviously a reader—but didn't go so far to pull one out.

"You read a lot of non-fiction. And most of it's history."

"There's a lot we can learn from the past. And it's genuinely interesting. You can't make up what people went through to get us to where we are."

"True." she said, taking a sip of wine and touching one of the books—the *Autobiography of Eleanor Roosevelt*. "Though I admit, I wouldn't have seen a surfing dude reading history."

"Thought you said we were more than what our jobs are."

"I did. Also, was she as amazing as I've heard? She was a diplomat and activist, right? Besides being the first lady."

"She was pretty incredible." Lando came over and bumped Jonathan and he rubbed the dog's ears. "Eleanor fought for the rights of minorities when few were, in some pretty unique ways. I use political figures like her, like Ella Baker, to engage—" he stopped, realizing what he'd almost said, that he used these famous women's stories to engage his female students.

LYING, BAKING, & SURFING

"Surfers? What can they learn from Ella Baker?" She raised her eyebrows at him.

He had the strongest desire to point over her shoulder and go, "What in the world is that!?" And then hope that distracted her. He never should've lied. But how would he tell her the truth now? She'd wonder what else he lied about and leave him. But at some point, she'd want surfing lessons, at his imaginary surf shop.

"Breena, I need—"

She startled, put down her wine, and reached for her phone. "Oh good," she said, reading off the screen. "Matt is apparently out of the hospital. Oh, that makes me feel so much better." She flung her arms around his neck. Then pulled back with a laugh. "Sorry. I think the alcohol is going to my head."

"Matt?"

"Remember, my . . . friend's friend? The one in a car accident. Hattie just texted to say he's out of the hospital."

"Oh good." He sat down on the couch, and she joined him, facing him with her leg drawn up next to her. "How do you know Hattie?" He needed to tell her the truth, he knew that. He just couldn't bring himself to do it.

"Oh . . . just one of those things," she said, dropping her eyes and playing with the hem on her skirt. "She . . . um . . . I used to work with her. Before I owned my . . . yeah . . . but she's an old coworker."

"At the winery?"

What had happened to the evening? Breena now seemed nervous. She reached behind her to grab her glass and downed half her wine. He searched for something to save the evening.

"Oh! I wanted to book a class in your yoga studio. One evening or an early morning. What's the name of your place? I'll check out the schedule. You guys have beginner classes, right?"

She bit her lip and nodded. "I just . . . there's a lot going on

139

right now and . . . I'm going to be honest. I don't want to talk about work or old coworkers or anything like that. I mean seriously," she continued. "I know I keep saying this, but our jobs don't define us! I mean, aren't we past the day where our last names are tailor, thatcher, and hunter?"

Her eyes were glistening with tears, begging for him to listen to her. Maybe her yoga studio was going under, and she didn't know how to fix the problem, or she had to sell it to a competitor and didn't want to. Or she had a business partner, maybe Hattie, that was causing a lot of problems for her.

Either way, it didn't matter tonight.

Jonathan stepped forward and brushed her hair from her eyes, staring down at her. He cupped her chin and kissed her—gentle, but sweet and lingering. "Yes. We are more than our jobs," he told her.

She closed her eyes, and a tear leaked out. "Tonight, I need to be more than just my occupation and how I make money to survive."

In response, he put on some slow jazz and tugged her up off the couch, wrapping his arms around her and moving in a slow sway. Breena set her head on his shoulder and pressed her body into his. He wanted her to make the first move, but as the song ended and another came on, it was getting harder to concentrate. She smelled so good, the cinnamon and vanilla reminding him of Sunday morning cinnamon rolls. Her body was warm in his arms and fit perfectly against him.

Jonathan forced himself to relax and take things slowly. He needed to enjoy this moment and not rush on to the next one. But that idea flew out the window when Breena moved her head and kissed him, her tongue darting into his mouth.

twenty-four

JOHNNY'S roving hands landed on her butt, cupping and lifting her closer to him. She let out a little squeal, and he chuckled into her mouth. He smelled of the ocean, sand, and salt. She wondered if his love of surfing and the ocean was in his blood, a part of his very essence. Then stopped thinking as he pushed her against the wall and began kissing her intensely. Instinctually, she wrapped her legs around his waist, grinding against him, feeling him press against her core. God, she'd never thought she was flexible enough to wrap her legs around someone, but somehow Johnny made it possible. Heat and lust coiled in her belly as he moved his lips down her neck, nibbling on the sensitive skin. She was so aroused, and the night had barely begun.

The slow jazz music changed to something faster, seeming to match the heat building between them. His hand found bare skin on her back, making her gasp from the feel of skin on skin. Somehow, though he never stopped nibbling on her neck, and he'd pressed her against the wall, he unhooked her bra. Letting her legs drop and teasing him, she pulled his shirt off, mindful of his new tattoo. She ran her hands up his muscular chest, taking her time as he closed his eyes, enjoying the moment.

"God, your skin is so hot," she murmured and let her tongue trace a line across his collarbone. He tasted of the ocean, like she knew he would.

Johnny's hands slid beneath her shirt again, stroking her breasts under her loosened bra. Sliding a palm beneath the silky fabric, he caressed her nipple—just the lightest touch, but it was enough to flood her core. At her gasp, his hands explored her breasts, rolling the nipples between his fingers before moving away to rove over her body, learning how she liked to be touched while his lips ravished her mouth.

The sensation of his hands and lips combined with the thrum of the music threatened to overwhelm her. Then her brain told her to stop thinking and turned off entirely.

Sabrina ripped her blouse off, tossing it to the floor, then wiggled out of her bra, ready to let it join her shirt. But at her feet, something let out a huff, and she yelped in surprise.

"Oh, Lando," she said, bending over to grab her shirt off his face where she'd accidentally dropped it. "I'm so sorry. I'd forgotten you were under us.

Lando let out a frustrated sigh before grumbling and climbing onto his doggy bed.

"He's ok. He'll get over it—he adores you," Johnny whispered into her ear, then nibbled on it, making her gasp.

She laughed, a quick puff of air. "Just Lando?"

He smiled and looked down at her breasts before cupping them. God, she could see the admiration in his eyes. She hadn't seen that from a man in a really long time.

"Not just Lando."

He kissed her, a deep kiss, running his hands up and down her back before taking her hand and drawing her up the stairs and into his bedroom.

* * *

She curled up next to him, her head on his chest, both of them breathing hard. Three orgasms to his one. Three! She'd experienced nothing like that before. Everything tingled, but her body felt heavy and loose.

Beneath her ear, Johnny's heart rate slowed.

"Good god," she murmured.

"I prefer Jonathan," he said. "Though if you want to refer to me as a god, feel free."

"Sounds like the beginnings of a horror movie." She deepened her voice, pretending to be a narrator in a movie preview. "After sex, the handsome hero transforms into a god, and then wrecks havoc on the nation, demanding the worship of the entire world. Only the girl—his true love—can bring him back to reality." She wiggled into his soft mattress and satiny sheets, reveling in the feel of his warm body under hers, his arm holding her close. "And if it's a porno, it takes sex to bring him back to reality."

"I think I've seen that one," he said, with a chuckle. He gently ran his hand up and down her bare back.

"I thought your name was Johnny," she said, relaxation making her voice heavy.

"Johnny, Jonathan. I'll answer to either." His own voice was tired, slurred.

She felt so relaxed, so loose, and at peace. A good date, ending with fantastic sex, was exactly what she'd needed. She ran her fingers up his arm, and he hissed.

"Sorry," she said. "Mine's sore too."

"Unhappy with the decisions of the day?"

He wasn't just asking about her jellyfish tattoo. She raised herself up on an elbow and pushed her hair from her eyes. "No. It's perfect. Today's been perfect." She kissed him, gentle and sweet and lazy.

"Me neither," he told her. She put her head back on his chest and closed her eyes. This moment, this day, this date was one of the best she'd ever had, and she was so happy she'd relaxed enough to enjoy it.

twenty-five

JONATHAN FELT RATHER than heard Breena slip out of his bed and tiptoe toward the bathroom. The toilet flushed and water ran in the sink. He waited for the sense of the mattress dipping, waited to feel her sliding in next to him, cuddle under the blankets, and curl one long bare leg around his. Maybe he'd roll over, give her a lingering kiss, and see what happened next.

But instead, he heard his bedroom door open and her footsteps pad down the stairs. Was she leaving without saying goodbye? He hadn't heard her pickup her discarded clothing, but maybe she'd done that while he was still asleep.

His heart dropped. Was she the type to just leave after the night they'd had? Even if she never wanted to see him again, she hadn't seemed the type to ghost him and sneak out in the middle of the night. The least she could do was give him some excuse about having to get up early before heading back to her life.

Jonathan curled around his pillow and strained for whispers of movement, the sound of water being poured into a glass, maybe the squeak of the creaky step as she came back to the bedroom. But there was nothing. Not even the puff of the front door opening. Lando started panting and Jonathan opened his eyes. The lab stood, nosed the door open, and went down the stairs, his claws noisy on the flooring.

Her voice floated up and through the open door, so quiet he had to strain to hear it. "Did you come down to keep me company? You did, didn't you? Such a good puppy," she said in that deep baby-voice everyone used with dogs.

Jonathan grabbed his phone to check the time—6:44 a.m. She must be an early person, one of those who felt the day was ruined if she didn't get up before sunrise. Or maybe his snoring had kept her awake. Or maybe she hadn't enjoyed lying in bed with another person. Or maybe she was regretting last night and trying to figure out if she could leave without waking him.

He threw his pillow over his face; he needed to stop overthinking everything. He'd never obsessed like this about another woman.

"Are you supposed to be on the couch?" her voice filtered up.

No, Lando wasn't, but he'd never been able to teach the giant black lab that he wasn't actually a lap dog.

"Ok, I guess it's fine, if you're cuddling," she continued. "Just try not to drool on Johnny's t-shirt."

That was a good sign—she was still wearing the Metallica t-shirt he'd offered for her to sleep in. She hadn't changed into her own clothes, and probably wasn't planning to leave. Tugging up the blanket and turning over to get comfortable, he tried to drift back to sleep, but his internal clock told him to get up or he'd be late for work.

His internal clock needed to learn what weekends were. Stupid work. Always controlling every aspect of his life. Couldn't even have a lazy Sunday morning of sleeping in until eight.

He flipped over a few times, hoping to snooze, before finally giving up. Pulling on a pair of running shorts and a Dave Matthews Band t-shirt, he went downstairs.

Breena's hair was mussed around her face, the strands gleaming in the small light she'd turned on. She sat on his blue couch, her long bare legs on the coffee table, Lando's head on her lap, reading *The Autobiography of Eleanor Roosevelt*. The purples, oranges, and yellows in her jellyfish tattoo glowed as she stroked the dog's ears.

"Hope we didn't wake you," she said. "I think I'm too used to getting up early—couldn't sleep anymore."

He let out a yawn. "Yeah, me too. During the week, I'm usually up by now. Coffee?"

"Yes, please," she said. She put down the book and started to stand. Lando opened his eyes to glare at Jonathan. He didn't want her to move.

"Stay there," he said. "You both look so comfy. I'll bring it to you. Do you like cream or sugar?"

"Just a little cream or half-and-half or whatever, is fine, if you have it," she said.

Yawning, he went into the kitchen, pressed start on the coffee machine and grabbed mugs, cream, and spoons. Crossing back into the living room with her coffee, he noticed she'd gone back to the book.

"You can borrow that."

"Oh, thanks," she said, her eyes lighting up. "I like it so far. I was going to order a copy off Amazon as soon as I found my purse and phone."

He joined her on the couch, sipping his coffee, willing his brain to wake up. She looked so cute in his shirt, with Lando cozy on her lap.

"Do you want some breakfast?"

"I should get out of your way. Let you get going with your Sunday. I'll get dressed and head back to my place."

"Stay. For breakfast, at least. It's not a problem at all unless you want to go."

She smiled over her coffee. "I'd love to stay. I'm actually starving."

He ran through the list of food he had. Milk, sandwich makings, some frozen chicken, old vegetables and fruit and a box of Froot Loops. He needed to go grocery shopping; he couldn't offer Breena Froot Loops, even if it was vegetarian.

"We should order hot cross buns," he said. "I'll get them delivered. There's this amazing shop in Encinitas, been around forever."

"It's seven a.m.," she said. "Is anyone doing deliveries this early?"

"It's a bakery," he said. "Aren't they open by now?" Clicking on his phone, he realized he'd missed several text messages from yesterday, starting in the afternoon, all from the vice-principal at his school.

> Don't check your emails. These parents are getting out of control. We need to talk.

> Sorry to bug on a weekend, but I think we may need to have a conversation before Monday.

> I get it. Boundaries. Good for you. If possible, could we schedule a call for Sunday afternoon?

He shut down the thread without responding. It was the weekend, goddamnit. He was having a fantastic time. He was going to enjoy it, without work interfering. He'd deal with the parents trying to get him fired on Monday.

Breena was smiling at him, not picking up on his stress. "They do."

"They do what?"

"Bakers. They get up super early."

Oh right. Breakfast. His favorite hot cross buns from childhood. He pulled up the Grubhub app and started scrolling. "They're not in Grubhub," he said after trying various combinations of search words. "Unless I'm not remembering the name of the bakery." He kept swiping.

"What's the name?"

"I don't know, Sugar Happiness, Sweet Ecstasy. Something like that."

"Sugar Bliss?" There was a tightness to her voice that hadn't been there before, but when he glanced over, she was looking on her phone, frowning, Eleanor Roosevelt's biography forgotten next to her.

"That's it." He swiped through the Grubhub selections, not finding it. "Guess they're not in there. Bummer. We used to go there all the time when I was a child. Favorite Sunday treat."

"The owner probably hasn't even considered Grubhub as a way to bring in revenue."

He grimaced, finding another bakery that delivered cinnamon rolls. He supposed they were close enough. He'd have to stop by the bakery, maybe next time Breena spent the night.

"Next time," she said, echoing his thoughts. "I'll get them for you next time."

His heart soared, though he kept his face buried in his phone. She wanted a next time. They'd have breakfast together again, presumably after another fun night.

"What's your plan for today?" she asked after he'd placed the order and refilled their coffees.

He should be doing his laundry, getting some groceries,

checking his work emails, grading papers, preparing lesson plans, and basically getting ready to have a smooth week.

But he said, "I have nothing. What about you?"

"Well, I should get out of your way, shower and get some chores done," she said, which was odd, because she hadn't seemed like the type to use a weekend to prepare for the week. She seemed more like the, 'I ran out of underwear and there's no food, so I will run to the store at midnight,' kind of type.

You know, the opposite of him.

"But..." she said, drawing it out.

"But?"

"But I was thinking." She grinned, pushing her hair from her eyes. "I'm not looking forward to chores around the house. And the weather is going to be nice. Not too hot with some clouds and fog. What if we take a picnic lunch up to Temecula and do a hike? I just heard about an easy one, that's supposed to be really pretty."

"Actually that does—"

"It's ok to say no," she interrupted. "I mean that. Spending a weekend together is a lot. I mean, we got tattoos yesterday and . . . you know. Everything else. Which was really nice."

"It was."

She leaned forward and kissed him, tasting of coffee and lazy mornings. Her phone buzzed, a text message probably, and she pulled away to glance at it. Her face closed off, and she tossed it next to her on its side.

"A hike sounds good," Jonathan said. Her phone buzzed again. "Unless you have something."

"Nope," she said, firmly. "The day is yours. It's a Sunday. And I'm doing what I want. And I want to spend it with you."

twenty-six

JOHNNY PULLED his Jeep into the lot at the Dripping Springs Campground, parked and went around to pull a backpack full of water and snacks out of the trunk.

Sabrina glanced at her phone and took five cleansing breaths. The forty-minute drive up the 15 to Temecula had been pretty, but she hadn't enjoyed it. In fact, the drive had been horrible, not because of Johnny, but because of her phone. It had vibrated the entire drive; text messages and finally phone calls from various members of the board or the executives at Thinkfling coming through constantly. And she'd spent the entire time trying to keep up flirty banter with Johnny, ignoring the constant buzzing, reassuring him that everything was ok; that she didn't need to answer her phone or cancel their plans. It was the weekend, and no one needed her that badly.

She wasn't sure he believed her. She didn't believe herself.

And yes, she wanted to be the CEO of Thinkfling; she had fought and dreamed of it for years! All that sacrifice, those late nights, weekend hours, and stress. She'd lost hobbies, friendships, and time she'd never get back trying to fight her way up the ladder at Thinkfling. Heck, her obsession with the damn company had destroyed her marriage. And at the time, she'd thought it was worth it. Worth it to be like her mother, make a difference for other companies employing hundreds of people.

Her phone buzzed again; one of the board members offering to take her out to happy hour this afternoon.

Why couldn't they just wait until Monday to offer her, her life's dream?

It buzzed again, and she groaned, almost turning it off, but Nixi's face popped up.

> Hey girl, how'd it go last night?

Sabrina had to chuckle. She responded with a quick:

> Haven't been home yet and now we're up in Temecula going for a hike.

> Wow, you go! I just got home.

> Gonna take a nap. Didn't get any sleep. 😴

She added an emoji sticking its tongue out.

> And totally worth it. 😜

Another text messaged buzzed in—one of the executive's assistants, asking if she was available this evening for a dessert and coffee:

> Just to chat and catch up.

> Thinkfling is blowing up my phone!

She texted to Nixi.

LYING, BAKING, & SURFING

> You know what they're like. There's a price to being the CEO. Look, let's talk before you accept. I love you and want you to make the right decision. But I'm too hung over to think right now.

> Love you too. We'll talk tomorrow. I won't decide anything today.

> Have fun on your hike. That teacher needs a stress-free day. He's having a rough time. Kaito was telling me all about it. Sounds terrible. Did you know they work together?

That was the second time Nixi had thought Johnny was a teacher.

> Johnny's not a teacher. He owns a surf shop.

There was no response.

That was weird. Maybe she meant a surf teacher. But Kaito was a high school teacher, a math one. They'd chatted about it over drinks before the concert. Maybe she'd misunderstood or wasn't remembering right. But she could've sworn—

Her phone buzzed; another request for happy hour drinks that evening. With a growl of frustration, she stuffed it into the glove box. Tonight, she'd return all the calls and set up the meetings. And make a decision.

"You coming?" Johnny asked.

"Yep. Sorry!" Grabbing her own backpack with sunblock and water, she got out of the car. Birdsong surrounded the parking lot, and she could see orange poppies poking up through the grass just outside the lot. It was a good day to hike. Temecula was north of San Diego, a mountain town full of wineries. It was warmer here than in San Diego, but fog from the coast and a cool breeze promised it would stay bearable. She hadn't hiked since college, and now that she'd left her phone behind, she was excited to get into nature and spend the day with Johnny.

"Ready?" she asked him. He tossed something she couldn't see into the trunk, his face tight, and closed it up.

"Ready," he said. "We've got plenty of water and snacks. Let's see how far we get."

"Perfect."

Passing out of the parking lot and paying the small fee, they started up the trailhead. Within a few minutes, Sabrina's calves were burning, though they had gained little altitude. She wasn't used to walking on dirt, only on the treadmill at the gym. Watching her footsteps, she focused on making sure she wouldn't step in a hole and turn an ankle.

Thirty minutes in, they paused beneath an alder tree to drink some water. Poppies and various purple, yellow, and white flowers stuck their heads out of the grass. Butterflies kissed the flowers and dragonflies buzzed past. Sabrina wished she'd brought her phone for pictures, but it was what it was. Maybe she could come back here sometime, maybe with a professional camera. Maybe she'd even take a class on how to take nature pictures; she'd always wondered how a picture of trees could express so much emotion.

Not if you become the CEO, her internal voice whispered. She hushed it and pushed away the thought. She was not going to think about anything else. Just the hike and the day with Johnny.

"It's so peaceful," she said, looking around at the scenery. This year hadn't been super rainy, so there wasn't a wildflower bloom, but the flowers were trying. She bent close to examine some; she didn't know there were so many different types of purple wildflowers. Bird song, the wind in the trees, and the shuffle of their feet were the only sounds. Her heart slowed and the anxious warring voices inside, one telling her she'd be a fool not to take the CEO job, and the other screaming she'd be a fool to let go of her current lifestyle, quieted. Relaxation spread from her heart out. This was why people went hiking. This moment of peace. Of balance with the universe.

Johnny let out a sigh next to her. "God, this was a brilliant idea," he said. "Perfect day to get away from all the chaos. Ready to keep walking?"

"Ready," she said.

They went a little further; the trail climbing. Sabrina was glad for the thick fog. There was no shade on this trail and if it had been sunny, they would've been boiling. As it was, sweat dripped down her back and wet her forehead. At the peak of the incline, a large rock split the path in two. There was no route marker. Each trail looked to be about the same width, one heading into some trees, the other into grass.

"Maybe we should've grabbed a map," Sabrina said.

"I'm not sure it's necessary here," Johnny said. "The path probably just splits and reconnects further up." He drank noisily from his water bottle. "So, what direction should we go?"

She pretended to flip a coin. "Left," she said.

"How do you know?"

"I don't," she said with a shrug. "It's a guess. But what's the worst that happens? If it doesn't feel right, we follow the trail back."

"Sounds like a plan," he said.

A raindrop hit the dirt in front of them. "I didn't think it was supposed to rain today," she said.

"It wasn't, which means it's just a bit of California drizzle."

Good. She was having too much fun to head back to the car and her phone. She wondered how many messages were waiting for her and then pushed the thought away. "Oh, that's perfect," she said. "It'll keep us cool."

"You sure?" Johnny asked as more drops splattered down. "You never know; might be a bit more than drizzle."

"I think we'll be okay. A little rain won't hurt us. We're heading through the trees. We can stand under one if it gets too bad."

* * *

An hour later, Sabrina flicked water from her eyes. They were completely lost. Not only were they lost, but the ground and the "path" they thought they'd been following was nothing more than a cesspool of mud. She was soaked through, her expensive tennis shoes ruined and her socks so wet, she was getting blisters. Worst of all were the huge raindrops that hurt when they hit bare skin. And there was no sign the rain was going to stop soon.

She'd never been more miserable; not even when Thinkfling had almost missed a deadline, and she'd stayed up for 38 hours straight. Not when she signed her divorce papers. Not when she'd fallen in high school and broken her wrist. This moment was one of the worst of her entire life.

Johnny stopped and squinted up at the sky. "Ok," he said. "I'm calling it. I have no idea where the car is."

"And I can't believe we both left our cell phones in your car," Sabrina snapped.

The universe wasn't just an asshole, it was a bastard too.

twenty-seven

"WE'RE NOT LOST," Sabrina said, flicking water out of her eyes and wishing she'd bothered to wear a hat. "This is Temecula. People don't get lost in Temecula. We're not back-trail hikers planning to camp out under the stars. We hiked for a whole hour, along a trail! Listen for the traffic on the 15 for god's sake. It's one of the worst freeways in the state. That'll tell us which way to go."

"Well, let's pull out our phones and use a map, or a compass app or something," Johnny snapped. "Or call for help. Oh wait, we both left our phones in the car!"

They were standing under a tree, which helped reduce the heavy, almost painful rain to a spring trickle. And while beneath the tree was better than trying to find a path between the bushes, while being blinded by the rain, the muddy water was rising around their feet. They'd have to move soon.

Sabrina pulled the collar of her sweatshirt up, trying to keep the rain from running down the back of her neck. "Why'd you leave your phone?" she asked. "It didn't even occur to me to wonder if you had yours. We were going hiking—we could've gotten lost. And we actually did!"

"Same question," he retorted. "Why would you leave yours in the car?"

"I wanted the fucking thing gone! I wanted to have a good weekend before I went back to working ninety-hour work weeks. People needed to leave me alone, and they just kept calling and texting!" She was screaming now, yet the patter from the rain seemed to absorb it. "And I couldn't think. They didn't care what I wanted, and they weren't listening."

Johnny shook his head, staring down at the muddy water. "I get that," he said softly. "I'm so tired of people not listening to me, either."

"Why can't people just leave us alone to do what we want?" Sabrina asked. She swiped at the water or tears on her face with a chilly hand. "Is that why you left your phone? Because people wouldn't leave you alone?"

"Kind-of. They're just accusing me of stuff I didn't do," Johnny muttered. He took off his hat and flicked water from the brim before putting it back on.

"Accusing you of stuff?" Sabrina asked, a shiver snaking up her spine. "What kind of stuff?" Was he being accused of . . .? Oh my god. Sabrina felt sick.

"It's not what you're thinking," Johnny said. "I may have . . . I don't own my own surf shop. I'm actually a high school teacher and the parents are trying to get me fired."

"For what?" Sabrina whispered.

"One of my students committed suicide." He said it softly, so softly she shouldn't have been able to hear it over the rain. Yet it was like he'd shouted it.

Sabrina gasped, her hands over her mouth. "That's horrible."

"I know it wasn't my fault," Johnny continued. "But I felt responsible, so I started a suicide support group. I asked the school board for permission and had a counselor attend. It went great. But some of the parents took offense, claiming talking about it could cause suicide. They were scared; I know that. Suicide can be contagious around teenagers—they don't understand it's forever." He rubbed the spot between his eyes. "But what really pissed them off was when the LGBTQ+ club started attending. So now they're working really hard to get me fired and must have done something this weekend, because the vice principal wants to set up a meeting before Monday classes start. Oh, and my name is Jonathan, not Johnny. Johnny was who I was pretending to be when I was just a cool surfer dude."

Though she was tired, so cold she shivered, and so wet her fingers were wrinkled, her heart went out to Johnathan. "I'm sorry you had a student commit suicide. And the parents' response is to try to get you fired? That's terrible."

"More terrible for her family. But these parents are all over social media, pulling apart random things I've said in my classes and taking it out of context. And the last text message I got from my vice principal said they're setting up a meeting with my union rep too, which doesn't mean good things. Probably suspension with pay while they do an 'investigation.'" He said the last word with finger quotes.

"So, you lied about who you were?"

"It just slipped out," Johnny said. "I was listening to my favorite podcast—Weird Rants—and the host was talking about how she pretends to be someone else on plane rides. And it sounded like fun."

What the hell? Had they actually been listening to the same podcast at the same time?

"I'm sorry," Johnny continued. He wiped at his eyes. "I didn't mean to lie. It just got out of hand. I'm not some crazy person. I'm just a bit broken right now."

Sabrina reached out to shake his damp hand. "Hi, my name is actually Sabrina, not Breena. I was the Chief Strategy Officer for a small marketing firm called Thinkfling. I worked sixty and seventy-hour weeks. The CEO fired me a few weeks ago. Because I got bored and the idea of day-drinking and binge-watching Netflix sounded terrible, I got a job at a bakery, kneading dough and selling baked goods. I've been trying to be more easygoing, reading books on how to go with the flow and be in the moment. I'm trying to listen to what the 'universe is telling me.'" She was the one to use quote marks now. combined with an eyeroll. "Honestly, I'm just trying to heal from the trauma." She met his eyes, hers filling with tears. "I'm divorced because I put my job above everything else. My phone's been blowing up because the board fired the CEO, and they want me to be the next one. I don't know if I want to accept, but they're not leaving me alone to think. So, I left my phone in the car."

"We both lied about who we are," Johnny said. "I don't know if that's a good thing."

Sabrina knew what he meant. They should be laughing about how similar they were, forgiving the other because they "got it" but instead she was wondering what else he might have lied about. Judging from how he stared down at the ground, his lips tight, he was thinking the same thing.

Johnny shifted his feet. The muddy water was starting to cover his shoes. "We should go. The water is rising, but I think the rain's lightening up."

And it was. Rather than a downpour with thick drops that splashed off leaves, the rain had turned into a heavy shower. Sunlight peeked through a break in the clouds, making the forest glitter.

"I take it you're not a yoga-loving-meditator?" Johnny asked.

"Nope." She took a step out from under the tree overhang. They needed to move and find the car or another person before it got dark. "I'm the opposite of free-spirited. I'm intense, driven, and probably narcissistic. I have perfectionism and control issues. The other day it took me three hours to buy a pair of shoes for work. I had to read all the reviews, do comparisons, read more reviews. I was considering a spreadsheet to compare them but thought that might be too much."

Johnny followed her out from under the tree. The rain was definitely getting lighter, and the burst of sunlight made it easier to see.

"Ok, let's see if we can find the car," Sabrina said. "It has to be around here somewhere. Let's head that way." She pointed to a direction she thought they hadn't tried.

Or at least there was a tree that didn't look super familiar.

"How do you know we should go that way?" he asked, shouldering his backpack, and stepping onto what might have been a trail.

"I don't. Honestly, I'm just trained to make decisions that sound good and accept the consequences when they're incorrect."

"I can't believe you're some paper-pusher in administration."

"Technically, I'm not. I'm a baker." She wanted to tell him she couldn't believe he was a teacher, but when she thought about it, a teacher was the perfect job for him; he was gentle, compassionate, and patient. His condo full of history books fit him perfectly and even his love of horror movies made sense. She wished she'd met him when she was in a healthier place. There might have actually been something there.

Sabrina squinted. "I got it! That's the rock." She pointed up ahead. "The one we went the wrong direction from."

Jonathan laughed without humor. "We're coming from the opposite direction of where we started. We must have gone in a full circle."

"Least we found the path," Sabrina said. The ribbon of mud back to their cars looked amazing, even as the sun went back behind a cloud and the rain picked up again. She flicked the water from her eyes. "Let's get to the car."

Shouldering their backpacks, and squinting against the rain, they moved quickly, not stopping for drinks of water or to stare at the views. They got back to the car much faster than it had felt when they were going up the hill. Naturally, once at Jonathan's car, the rain slowed and stopped.

Sabrina rolled her eyes. "Nice timing universe."

"The universe is an asshole," Jonathan muttered. Two hours ago, she would've giggled, but now everything was different. They'd gone from a meaningful "we-really-like-each-other" to a heavy "now-what?"

They dried off as best they could, using a single sandy towel from Johnny's trunk and without saying a word, got into the Jeep. Jonathan grabbed his phone, settled into the driver's seat and lips tight, read a bunch of messages before sending a text, while Sabrina set up an early breakfast meeting with the board at Thinkfling for Monday morning. They were completely silent on the drive back. What was there to say? They'd both lied about who they were. And neither of them was what the other one had been attracted to.

Jonathan pulled up in front of her house. "The Tesla had always confused me," Jonathan said, looking at her car in the driveway. "It didn't seem to fit with your persona, but now that I know you're an exec, it makes sense."

"Sounds like we both have a lot going on," she said.

"Sounds like," Jonathan said, his arms folded and looking at the road in front of him.

"I had a wonderful time," she said. "Truly."

"Today was horrible," Jonathan said. "I can't believe we got lost in the mountains in Temecula. It's ridiculous."

"Ok, today sucked," Sabrina said with a small laugh. "But it'll be a good story one day." She leaned over to kiss his cheek. "Every date we had were some of the best of my life."

"Mine too," Jonathan said. His face softened and he reached over to brush a lock of damp hair off her forehead, tucking it behind her ear. "Look. It was an emotional day. We found out a lot about each other that was . . . surprising. But I would still like—"

"Let's just leave it at the but—" Sabrina said. "And delete the rest after. We both thought we were someone else, someone we thought would help us. Honestly, we're probably not in healthy places right now for a relationship. I'm a bit broken and you said you were too."

Jonathan rubbed the back of his neck. "I guess."

"But I'll be in touch when I get healthier." She awkwardly patted his shoulder and climbed out of the car.

"Are you going to take the job at Thinkfling? Become their CEO?" he called after her before she could close the door.

"Are you going to fight the parents for your job and your students?"

twenty-eight

MONDAY MORNING, Sabrina watched a Southwest airplane heading to San Diego International Airport fly by the conference room windows at Thinkfling. It had always amused her to see the reactions of those unprepared for the sight as the brain went through "oh my god, is that a plane?", "is that plane going to hit us?", and "what idiot designed their flight path between the buildings in downtown San Diego?"

But today, no one twitched or even looked at the plane; the board and the other C-level executives from Thinkfling were too focused on what they were trying to convince her to do. They'd already given Sabrina the compensation packet and because she wasn't an idiot, Sabrina had said she would negotiate it. But it was a fantastic offer, even before negotiations, and unless she went insane and bought a giant yacht and multiple homes in Europe, she'd never have to worry about money again. In fact, after a year or two, she'd be able to afford an ocean view property in La Jolla.

But today wasn't about the offer; it was about the future plans for Thinkfling. According to Gabriela, a Hispanic woman wearing an ice-blue business suit, and the president of the board, the board had been unhappy with the former CEO, for some time. Though Gabriela was an experienced speaker, her apology to Sabrina for her unapproved termination came off rehearsed and insincere.

Or maybe Sabrina was just jaded.

But Gabriela hadn't spent much time on the apology. The focus of the meeting was to tell Sabrina how amazing she was and then explain the new direction they wanted Thinkfling to go. A direction they said they needed her help with.

There were lies and exaggerations in their fawning over her, and their ideas for the future were too hastily put together and lacked implementation strategies. Or even genuine possibilities. Sabrina was savvy enough in office politics to tell the difference. But their plan, assuming the board and execs were fully invested, was exciting too. Gabriela talked about a full rebrand, a new mission statement, new goals, and new intentions for the business. There was talk of a whole new human resources revamp, which the human resources director offered Sabrina a tight smile about, that focused on remote work and work/life balance. No more expectations of the salaried staff to work sixty and seventy-hour weeks, no more expectations of work to be done after five p.m. for most of the staff—One of the board members interrupted— "Don't worry, Sabrina, we know you won't work that way."

Then they all laughed.

Sabrina forced a laugh with the rest of them, feeling like an over-the-top villain in a bad movie.

"But that comment left a bad taste in my mouth," she told Nixi when they met over drinks that evening at Boundaries. The normally twenties music was different tonight; a soft classical instrumental that soothed Sabrina's nerves. "Their laugh left a bad taste."

"Do you think the plan, their new ideas, are real?" Nixi

asked. "Cuz I'm all about that work/life balance right now. I'm working crazy hours trying to clean up the mess from Thomas leaving."

"I don't know." Sabrina thanked the bartender for their gin drinks, plucked the cucumber garnish, and bit into it. She was starving and couldn't wait for her burger. At least she didn't have to pretend to be vegetarian anymore. "I think some of the board members like the ideas, but not all of them. And I think with the right person guiding it, their plans might work, but I'm not sure the other execs are on board. I may have to clean house to implement these plans, which isn't the end of the world."

"But . . ." Nixi dragged the word out, proving she knew Sabrina had misgivings.

"But they want to change an entire culture that may not want to be changed. And I KNOW them. The second the work isn't done, or a deadline is missed, they won't accept work/life balance as an excuse. It'll be "all-hands-on-deck," "stagger schedules so not to pay the OT, but have people work round the clock," and "buy the team bagels, but not breakfast sandwiches because those are too expensive, but keep working them!""

"But you'll be the CEO. You can tell those people to go to hell."

"No, I can't. I need the board and the other execs to make these ideas work or there will be too much division. So, there's going to be compromise. Thomas wasn't the only one on that team driving the ridiculous hours and expectations. There were those who supported him, who thought if you want to get ahead, you need to work really long hours to make that happen."

Nixi leaned forward to sip at her cocktail, her long dark braids falling forward. "So, what do you want to do?"

"I have to accept the CEO position. I've sacrificed so much

to get to this point." Sabrina stirred her drink. "Maybe all this learning I've been doing with going with the flow, being more in the moment, will help. I can guide Thinkfling to a healthier place. Maybe these last few weeks haven't been a waste, and it actually was the universe trying to guide me. Maybe this is exactly where I'm supposed to be."

"Maybe." Nixi tapped her nails on the bar. "But you're such a different person than you were. I like this Sabrina. She's fun. She looks younger, she smiles and laughs. She went out on dates. She got a tattoo! The Sabrina I knew who was the Chief Strategy Officer for Thinkfling would've never done that stuff. I'm not sure this Sabrina would've sacrificed her marriage and family for a job."

"Those sacrifices got me here. Got me the offer of CEO," Sabrina sighed and pressed her forehead into the bar, the universal banging her head against a desk. "Well, hopefully I can keep a part of that Sabrina. I liked her too."

Nixi sighed and changed the subject. "How are things going with Johnny?"

"We broke up," Sabrina said. She raised her head off the bar, finished her drink, and waved the bartender over for another. She explained to Nixi about the hike and how she and Johnny had found out both of them were pretending to be someone they weren't. "I thought he could show me how to be more easygoing, that the universe had presented him to me. And he'd thought the same thing about me. Ridiculous and stupid."

"So, you're done."

"Yep. His name is Jonathan, for god's sake. Not Johnny. He was just trying out someone else, just like I was. Because we listened to the same podcast, and it sounded like fun. Completely ludicrous. And the timing is horrible. I have to focus on Thinkfling, and he's got a terrible situation at work. Not a good time for us to begin a relationship." She compartmentalized her emotions, pushing away her sadness about losing Johnny—Jonathan. It amazed her how easy it was to slip back into her corporate skin and the corporate behaviors of pushing aside her emotions. "How are things with Kaito?"

"So far, so good," Nixi said accepting the change of subject. "I've got plans to see him on Wednesday. We'll see where it goes. I'm being real careful this time; don't want him to hurt me again."

"Probably a good idea. You know how these teacher types are."

"Scalawags, all of them," Nixi said with an eyeroll. "But anyways, just think before accepting the CEO position. I think you might be jumping in too fast."

"Already accepted. I'll tell Hattie tomorrow; she texted while I was in that meeting that she fixed the oven at Sugar Bliss and would like me back in the morning. Apparently, she has new recipes and ideas she'd like to try."

"Want me to go with you?"

"Well, I start at 4:30 a.m. I know you don't want to get up that early."

"Nope," said Nixi.

"But maybe I'll go in, do my baking, and then quit at the end of my shift. That way she's not expecting me and then can't get anything done before she opens."

"You're a good person. How about I come by at one? You can save me a hot cross bun."

"Don't you have a job?"

"I got in an in with the new boss," Nixi said, with a flip of her braids.

Sabrina laughed. "Then yes, I could use the moral support. I like Hattie and want to make this easy on her."

"Then I'll be there."

twenty-nine

"TWO STONE IPAS, PLEASE," Jonathan asked the bartender and carried the two beers, foam spilling down the sides, to where Kaito sat on a barstool overlooking a sidewalk in the touristy part of Encinitas. Sun-drunk tourists in shorts, flip-flops, and bathing suit cover-ups passed in front of them, looking for bars or fish tacos after a long day at the beach.

"Thanks," Kaito said, taking a long pull from the beer. "So, you have classes tomorrow, right? You're done being suspended?"

"Back at work tomorrow, unless they tell me differently tonight," Jonathan said. "But they did temporarily shut down the suicide support group until things 'cool down.' Their words, not mine."

"That sucks," Kaito said. "Your group was doing a lot of good."

"If students still need support, they can go see a counselor both on or off site," Jonathan parroted after draining half his beer. "I'm also to be 'aware of what I say' in the classroom, understanding 'it might get taken out of context.' Oh! And because it's a 'hot-button topic,' admin has recommended I move or even cancel my unit on the Tulsa Massacre until things cool down. Their words, again."

Kaito groaned. "I hate it when admin tries to control what we teach. They're not teachers."

Jonathan drank more of his beer, feeling depressed. "We teach to make the kids pass tests so we get funding, let's be honest. No matter how much we dress it up, that's what we do. We're not teaching them to think anymore." He finished his beer, catching a hint of the ocean on his skin. He'd spent the day surfing at Moonlight Beach and had found momentary balance and peace riding the waves. But whenever he returned to his regular life, the peace, that balance disappeared, and he found he was more of a mess than before.

Well, he'd found the same peace with Breena—Sabrina, but that was done now.

Seeming to read his thoughts, Kaito asked. "Any word from Sabrina?"

"No. It's been two weeks now. I assume she's the CEO of whatever that company was, and everything is going as she wanted it." And how she wanted her life was without him being a part of it. He contemplated getting another beer. "How's Nixi?"

"Busy. Haven't talked to her much lately but we have tickets to see a show at Moonlight Amphitheatre this weekend. We'll bring a picnic. Wanna go with us?"

The last thing Jonathan wanted was to be a third-wheel as the two lovers made out in front of him. "No thanks. I'm trying to take things really easy," he said. "I'm doing a lot of reading and thinking." He took a deep breath and said what he'd been thinking about for months, ever since Lily's suicide. "Maybe it's time for me to do something different."

"Like what?" Kaito asked. He'd been making eyes at two pretty twenty-somethings in bikini tops and shorts as they walked by. One of the girls, a redhead, turned to look back at Kaito and Kaito smiled. Jonathan waved a server over and ordered another beer, waiting until the girls passed. "What are you thinking?" Kaito asked returning to the conversation. "A leave of absence?"

"Exactly. A sabbatical. Just time to do some reflecting, take some classes on teaching and—" A lump formed, surprising him. "Decide if I still want to teach. I mean it. I think I might be done."

"Of course you still want to teach," Kaito said. "You're a good teacher. You love it, and the kids love you. I always hate having them come out of your class and then head to mine. They're all bright-eyed and then I destroy them talking about calculus." He finished his beer. "You're just going through a rough patch. And these parents are terrible. They always say during parent-teacher conferences, 'how is this going to benefit my kid? I didn't take calculus and I'm fine.' And then I have to figure out a way to explain to these parents that math teaches critical thinking and problem solving without insulting them. Though most of the time they don't know I'm insulting them, because they lack critical thinking skills. Am I right?" It was an old joke and Kaito thumped Jonathan on the back, but Jonathan didn't respond.

"I don't see teaching getting any better," Jonathan said. "The parents just keep getting worse and worse. And then I do all this reading on history, which I really like, and I can't even teach what I want to."

"Sounds like it's time for a reset, then," Kaito said. "A break might be the best thing for you. And you can surf every day while you figure out what you want to do. Go on disability for stress. Your doc will sign off on it once they find out about Lily."

"Yeah, Sabrina and I used to joke about me becoming a surf bum." In his heart, what he missed was Sabrina. But she wasn't who he thought she was. And she was too busy for him. He wasn't a business guy, but even he knew the first year of a CEO's job was vital to their success. She was probably working eighty-hour weeks at this point. There was no time for romance.

"Send her a text," Kaito said, reading Johnny's mind, yet again. "It's been two weeks since you talked. She can ignore it if she wants."

"I don't want to bug her."

"You're not," Kaito said. "She never said she didn't want to see you again. It's just a text. If she blocks or ignores you, you get your answer."

Jonathan picked up his phone and read the last text from her—a simple one confirming she was on her way to meet at the coffee place before they got their tattoos. He wondered if she still liked her tattoo, or now regretted it.

The server delivered his beer, and he took a long swallow. Without thinking, he typed:

> How's the tattoo?

thirty

"HEY THERE, CLOEY," Sabrina said as she stepped into Sugar Bliss. "Did you get my call?"

"For three dozen hot cross buns," Cloey said, reaching back for the six large white boxes set aside. "I did! Obviously." She chuckled. "Hattie says she wants to talk to you, by the way, so not to leave." Cloey hurried into Hattie's office while Sabrina shifted from heeled foot to heeled foot. She'd only gotten a few hours of sleep the night before and was feeling it.

Actually, she remembered the exhaustion of the twelve and thirteen-hour days a little too well. And today, of course, she had an early meeting with a new client that she knew would love these buns. And the rest of the team appreciated Hattie's treats too, especially the hot cross buns with the caramel drizzle.

This was the first time she'd set foot in Sugar Bliss since giving Hattie her notice. Sabrina had always been able to send Nixi or someone else, but today Nixi had called out with a cold, which meant Sabrina had to grab the treats for the meeting.

She looked around the bakery. She'd spent several weeks at this business, alternately being frustrated by Hattie and the customers, and then loving seeing her creations sold and enjoyed. Hattie had even taken some of her advice, removing the faded photos of baked treats, though the walls still needed a coat of paint.

Sabrina shifted her feet again, regretting her choice of heels. They looked good with her pinstriped suit but were too high and pinched her toes. She considered leaving and calling to give Cloey her credit card over the phone, but it felt wrong to reach over the counter, grab her boxes, and just leave without paying.

"Sabrina," Hattie said, coming out of her office and offering her an awkward hug. "I've been trying to catch you."

"I know," Sabrina said. "I've been so busy, but I appreciate you doing all these extra orders for me. I may have some catering things for you too, so will be in touch. Everyone just raves about your new stuff."

She knew she was speaking too quickly and felt bad she'd quit without giving two week's notice. It had put more pressure on Hattie than Sabrina had felt was fair, especially after Hattie had taken a chance on her poor baking skills. But Hattie had been surprisingly kind about Sabrina leaving without notice.

"I know you probably have some sort of meeting to get to," Hattie said. "But I wanted to see if I could schedule some time to talk. I've been trying some of your marketing tricks; we have a Facebook page now and I post on the neighborhood pages. It's been working a little. But I want to do more."

"Of course," Sabrina said, passing her corporate credit card over to Cloey. "Let me put you in touch with our sales team." But even as she said it, she knew there was no way Hattie could afford Thinkfling's rates. The woman had struggled to get the money together to fix the oven, for god's sake. But without some marketing help, Sugar Bliss wouldn't survive much longer. The bakery would be gone in six months and someone else, probably some franchise selling cookies or cupcakes or whatever the latest trendy baking thing was, would come in and take over the space. And then all that would be left of Sugar Bliss was 'that place with the great hot cross buns we went to on Sundays when we were a kid, but I guess it's gone now.'

And it would be too bad. Hattie was too good of a baker to be forced into closing her business just because she didn't know how to run it.

"Hattie, I know you can't afford Thinkfling rates, even our basic plan, but I've been thinking of starting a weekly meeting where business owners like you can network and learn ways to market. It would be free, and I could have one of my junior marketing people run it. They'd learn and you would too."

"I was hoping—" Hattie shoved her graying hair from her face. "I mean, I get it. You're super busy, but I don't know how to do any of this stuff. I mean, Cloey had to help with Facebook after I messed up our first page. And I don't have the time to learn how to do giveaways and punch cards and stuff."

The bakery went quiet, the only noise coming from the people on the sidewalk outside. "I can try to help," Cloey said. "But with school—"

"No, it's ok," Hattie said. "I totally get it. We'll stick with the social media for now. One step at a time. No need to reinvent the wheel."

Sabrina winced at the business clichés. "Maybe partner with the delivery apps—GrubHub, UberEats, and those companies," Sabrina said. "I was . . . with someone a few weeks ago, and he struggled to find a bakery that would deliver on a Sunday morning."

"Don't companies like that take a cut?" Hattie asked.

"Of course, but it may help you to expand your reach, get to customers you wouldn't normally get to. Since Covid, deliveries are a huge part of successful restaurants."

"How much of a cut do those companies take? I'm not sure I can raise our prices much more."

"I don't know, Hattie. You'd have to speak to one of their reps. You can probably sign up online, but I do have to go." Saying her goodbyes, Sabrina grabbed the boxes, put them in the passenger seat of her car and headed down the 5 through the morning traffic to Thinkfling's corporate office.

She played with her streaming music, trying to find the perfect background music, feeling unsettled. Hattie really did need the help, but Sabrina didn't have the time to help her. She tapped her chin. There was an idea here, something she could do, just out of her reach.

thirty-one

JONATHAN PUT down the hand he'd raised to wave at Sabrina, his heart dropping. Maybe she hadn't seen him between putting the bakery boxes in her car and walking around to the driver's side in her stiletto heels. She had seemed in a hurry, but he could've sworn she'd glanced his way.

But maybe not.

He'd sent a text to her two days ago, asking how her jellyfish tattoo was, and she hadn't responded. It probably was for the best if she hadn't seen him; it would seem like he was stalking her. Heck, maybe that's what she'd thought, and that was why she hadn't waved back.

His favorite coffee shop was closed for remodeling, but he remembered Sugar Bliss from his childhood; best cinnamon rolls he'd ever had. And a sugary treat sounded amazing today. In fact, he'd planned to get a dozen with his coffee, take them into work. He'd make sure his vice principal got one. She'd been very kind and understanding about him taking a leave of absence beginning at the end of this week. In fact, he only had two more days of work and then this entire terrible year would be behind him. He'd get about five months off between his leave and the summer break; plenty of time to figure out what he wanted to do next.

The bell on the door handle jingled as he stepped inside, the smell of yeast, sugar, coffee, and calories surrounding him. There was one person ahead of him, a tall gentleman collecting a large box and holding out his credit card. A woman with graying hair was saying, "I'm so glad you're better. I was really worried."

"Me too," the man rumbled. "Definitely a scary moment. And thanks for sending those buns to the hospital for me, too. I don't know if my daughter was happier to see them or find out I was going to be fine."

"I'm sure she was happier you were going to be okay."

Jonathan wondered if he should leave; this seemed like an intensely personal conversation with a regular customer. He could come by tomorrow to get cinnamon rolls. Heck, when he was on leave, he could come by every day if he wanted to, then go surfing. That actually sounded like an amazing way to spend his five months.

He cleared his throat and lightly tapped the display case, pretending he was inspecting the pastries inside, hoping the man and woman would realize he was there. Inside the case was a wide variety of cinnamon rolls, sticky buns, hot cross buns, and breads. His stomach rumbled.

"It's been a really rough year for my daughter," the gentleman continued. "Between the separation and Lily's death. But I think I've talked her into moving in with me until she can get her head back on straight."

Lily?

"That's good news," the woman continued. "I know that'll help you both to heal."

Another woman stepped out, college-age, wearing leggings and a beachy tank-top that made him think of Sabrina. "Can I help you?" she asked Jonathan, but Jonathan just stared at the gentleman. He knew him—it was Matt Dicing, Lily's grandfather.

Jonathan needed to get out of here before Matt spotted him. He leaned away from the display case just as Matt turned his head to look at him.

"Mr. Hawkins!" Matt said.

"Hi," Jonathan said. "I was—just picking up—my coffee place was closed—and I didn't—and I remembered cinnamon rolls here—and—"

"I never got to say anything at Lily's funeral," Matt continued, breaking into Jonathan's stumbling speech. "But Lily so loved your class. She didn't talk much to her parents at the end . . . we thought it was normal teenager stuff . . ." Tears in Matt's eyes were mirrored in Jonathan's. "But we did used to talk about your class. I love history and she would share what she learned with me." Matt paused to wipe his eyes. "She really loved your class," he repeated. "It made her think and I think it made her happy, or at least—" a muffled sob escaped, and Matt dropped his eyes.

"I know she loved history," Jonathan said, wiping away his own tears. "I just wished I'd seen the signs."

"Everyone missed them. She hid a lot of her pain. She was even seeing a therapist, and even the therapist didn't see the warning signs either. Our Lily was a great actress."

"Teenagers are good at that," Jonathan said, his voice wobbly.

"But I'm glad I saw you. I kept meaning to tell you—she really loved your class. And it wasn't your fault. It wasn't any of our faults." With a pat on Jonathan's back, Matt grabbed his box and left.

"Did you still—" the girl behind the counter asked, but Jonathan went outside, not even ordering the cinnamon rolls or coffee he'd come in for. Instead, he sat in his car and wept. That's what had been missing. Forgiveness. He'd needed someone from Lily's family to tell him it was ok. That he hadn't done anything wrong. That no one had done anything wrong. Lily was just hurting so much that suicide had seemed like the only way to make it stop.

He was craving the ocean, craving that moment of balance on the board, but knew he'd have plenty of time for it later. He took a deep breath and put his car into gear. He needed to get to school and then take some time to heal.

But now he knew he would.

thirty-two

SABRINA KICKED off her heels and paced in her office at Thinkfling, the industry carpet rough against her bare feet. She loved her giant CEO desk with its three computer screens, the tall windows that overlooked downtown San Diego, and the room to actually move, think, and plan.

But today, the size of her office didn't seem to matter. She couldn't figure out how Thinkfling could help business owners like Hattie, who had great products, but not the business knowledge to stay in business or the money to pay someone to do it for them. Thinkfling didn't want anything to do with the small businesses. A weekly marketing meeting for other owners to share ideas was fine and dandy but would do nothing for those hanging on by a thread, already tapped out on time and money.

Maybe she needed to come up with some sort of revenue sharing plan. If the business didn't make money, neither would Thinkfling. She could try it on a select few companies that were truly struggling and didn't have the bandwidth to do the work themselves.

But she knew the board and the other C-level executives

would never go for it; not with the financial outlay the rebranding and new mission statement was projected to cost them. There was no extra money to take on charity cases. But there had to be something she could do.

Sabrina kept circling her thoughts, scribbled on her white boards, and kept pacing. A chime went off on her phone. It was 5 p.m. She had emails to answer, an SBAR to proof, and a dinner meeting at 6:30. She didn't have the time anymore for this kind of thinking. She was the face of Thinkfling and needed to stop thinking of herself as the problem solver. She should throw how to help tiny struggling businesses at one of the marketing specialists, see if they could come up with a plan.

If she went to the board with this idea, they would tell her she couldn't save everyone; that businesses that were struggling may need to close. That businesses opening and closing was an important part of the local economy and while Sabrina knew it was true, it sucked for the small business owners that put their heart and soul into everything they did.

But god, doing this, going to a revenue-based model would be so interesting and so much fun. It would be challenging, but she would actually see if the marketing plans her team developed were actually working. She'd need buy-in from the business owner and the rest of the company to ensure every initiative would work or it would cost her.

It would cost her company. Her company.

Her Company.

HER COMPANY.

She wrote "Her Company" on the whiteboard and started a list:

- She still had savings from her divorce.
- She'd need to get a business loan.
- She'd need a business plan.

- She'd be able to help small businesses truly struggling with their marketing. Help them become sustainable. Help their owners achieve work/life balance goals.
- She wouldn't have a board or other executives to play office politics with.
- She could take Nixi with her.
- She would control her schedule, working as much or as little as she wanted.
- Starting a business was a lot of work. She could end up working more than she was now.
- But it would be the fun stuff she'd get to do.
- No more meaningless meetings.
- She could choose whom to bring in, not be stuck with dinosaurs set in their ways or too used to their corporate paycheck to want to try different things.
- She'd bring in marketing contractors, so she didn't have to worry about California Labor Laws.
- She'd give it a better name than Thinkfling, for god's sake.
- She'd have ultimate control and ultimate responsibility for mistakes.
- She would make mistakes, mistakes that might cost the entire company.
- Worst case, she could get another job.

Sabrina circled "another job." She'd done that before and it hadn't been the end of the world. She'd learned a great deal about baking and work/life balance when she was working with Hattie.

Her phone chimed again; she needed to leave to make the 6:30 dinner meeting she didn't care about. Sabrina stepped back and looked at the scribble on her whiteboard, took a picture with her phone, and erased the board so no one could see what she was contemplating. She'd transfer the information to her board in her home office.

She could do this. She and Nixi together could change the lives of tiny businesses that truly needed her help, not conglomerates looking to push into the San Diego markets.

She had no money for a start-up though, and she would need money to make this work.

* * *

After the boring and useless dinner meeting, Sabrina went home and wrote up her list, adding a few more ideas. Staring at the bullet points, she felt more sure of this than anything she'd ever done. She looked down at her jellyfish tattoo. Jellyfish went where the ocean, their universe, took them. They stayed in balance, or they died. She needed balance to be a part of the plan.

She stayed up all night putting the pieces together. Throughout it all, she felt calm and at peace, sure of her decision, even though she didn't know where to get the money from. In fact, she'd never felt this sure about anything in her life.

thirty-three

A WEEK LATER, Sabrina opened her front door to Nixi. "Thanks for coming over on a Saturday. I got the sticky buns from Sugar Bliss with the butterscotch drizzle."

"Oh my god," Nixi said, hurrying into the kitchen. "I've put on ten pounds since I found out about that bakery, but it's been totally worth it."

Sabrina poured her friend and assistant a cup of coffee and put a sticky bun on a plate in front of Nixi. The woman flipped her braids over a shoulder. "So, what's going on?" she asked, forking up a bite of the pastry. "What non-work, but work stuff did you have to talk to me about?"

"I have an idea I want to run past you," Sabrina said. She looked at the sunlight filtering in through her windows. "And it's going to take time and I couldn't talk about it at work."

"I'm excited," Nixi said. "I hope it's starting your own business."

Sabrina laughed. "Of course you knew," she said, as she started explaining her idea.

An hour later, Nixi was brainstorming on a pad of paper.

They'd filled up pages with ideas. "This could work," she concluded. "But it's a huge risk."

"But for small businesses that can't afford a marketing company, a revenue split ensures we do our part to help them achieve success," Sabrina said.

"But marketing is an art. You may do everything right and still lose money, especially if the business owner doesn't do their part. There needs to be buy-in. They need to invest in us, too."

"Good point," Sabrina said. She got up to pace, the bohemian skirt she wore on the weekends flaring around her ankles. "So, there needs to be a deposit. Or an upfront cost, but it needs to be less than companies like Thinkfling."

"Absolutely." Nixi scribbled on her pad of paper, circling a few words, and drawing an arrow.

"So you're on board?"

"Heck yeah," Nixi said. "When can I start?"

"I won't be able to pay you what you're currently making. Assuming I can even get a loan."

"Ask your mom for money. Offer her a percentage of a stake in the company. She has to be getting close to wanting to retire. This can give her something to do."

Sabrina expected to feel anxiety churn in her stomach, a hesitation about telling her mother she needed help. But instead, it felt like everything fell into place. Of course her mother was the solution. Her mother would be an amazing partner.

"That's a genius idea. But are you sure? Starting a business is hard. We might be working long hours."

"True, but I'm ok with that. And I'll make sure you don't work too long of hours, or you'll risk burn-out," Nixi said, flipping her braid over her shoulder.

Sabrina took a deep breath. "Ok, I'll call my mom. Tell no one."

"Of course not," Nixi said. She toasted Sabrina with her coffee mug. "To us and to starting a business."

"To us and to starting a business," Sabrina echoed, raising her own mug. They sipped their cold coffee and made matching faces at the taste of the bitter dregs. Nixi chuckled.

"I'm so relieved," Sabrina said. "This idea feels so good. So balanced and perfect. I've never been so sure of anything in my life."

"I know what you mean," Nixi said. She leaned back and forked up a final bite of sticky bun. "Speaking of balanced . . . Jonathan took a leave of absence from his job."

"He wasn't fired?"

"No. The school board concluded he did nothing wrong. But they made him suspend the suicide support group, and he was told he'd have other teachers auditing his classes at random times."

"Woooowwww," Sabrina said. "That's ridiculous. I can't believe the parents caused that much drama."

"So, he went out on a leave to figure out if he still wants to teach. Has lots of free time if you're looking for something to do on the weekends. And he'll help with your work/life balance." Nixi waggled her eyebrows.

"He texted me last week," Sabrina admitted. She stretched her arm out and looked at her jellyfish tattoo. She'd only grown to adore it more. "I didn't respond. We both lied about who we were. And I'm not what he wants. He wants a free-spirit, not a CEO, and soon to be business owner."

"A business owner who could be more relaxed. You were still you around him; just a different version."

"I still lied."

"So did he. But not about anything important. Just what

you both did for a living. Thought we were more than our jobs. They don't define who we are."

Sabrina took a sip of her cold coffee and made another face, getting up to pour them both new cups. "If it's meant to be, I'll run into him somewhere."

"No." Nixi took Sabrina's hand in both of hers. "The universe already smacked you upside the head when he texted you. That was the universe's way of telling you that things weren't done between you. Stop being an idiot and text him. Ask him to go out to coffee."

"But—"

"Stop thinking. Just do it. One coffee date doesn't mean you'll be together forever."

With a sigh, Sabrina reached for her phone. She re-read the text from Jonathan asking how her tattoo was. She began to type:

> My tattoo is good. All healed up. How's yours?

She pressed send.

"Ok, done," she told Nixi, showing her friend the screen.

"He's writing back," Nixi squealed, putting the phone on the table between them. They watched the three dots, which came and went for several minutes. Sabrina paced away, looking out into her backyard. "Come on, dude," Nixi said. "The suspense is killing me!"

That's good to know. Mine's good. Healed too, Nixi read. "Non-committal," she observed. "But he responded, that's a good sign." She looked down at the phone. "There's more dots."

The coffee in Sabrina's stomach seized up, and she felt faintly nauseous. "He sent a picture," Nixi said. Sabrina walked over to see Jonathan's tattoo—the wave she'd picked out for him. It had healed, the black and gray looking fresh and vibrant, the tiny details crisp.

> That looks good

> Thanks.

There weren't any more dots.

Sabrina looked to Nixi. "Now what?"

"Show him yours."

Sabrina took a picture of her tattoo and made a face. Enough with the dating games.

She took one deep yoga breath and typed out:

> Feel up to coffee or a cocktail tomorrow? Or hot cross buns? I know a great place.

She bit her lip and pressed send.

> I'd love that.

recipes

Thanks for continuing to read this far. If you're looking for author notes and thank yous to all the wonderful people in my life, those are after this section.

One of the best parts of writing this book was including recipes from the food I imagined Sabrina and Johnny enjoying. If you follow me on TikTok or Instagram, you can watch these goodies created, along with some of the mishaps. By the way, you'll find out I'm not a very good baker. But it was fun to try something different and stretch my creativity in this way.

If you try any of these recipes, tag me on my various social medias, especially on TikTok. I'd love to see how they come out!

hot cross buns

CINNAMON ROLLS and sticky buns (recipes below) are in every bakery, but hot cross buns are more unique. I mentioned these unique buns several times throughout the book. They are are Matt's favorite and he used them to try to bribe his daughter to visit more. Hattie brought them to him when he was hospitalized after the accident.

Hot cross buns were surprisingly difficult to make, with multiple rises, which is why Sabrina was beating herself up so much when she burned her first batch back in chapter 1.

Ingredients:

- 3 teaspoons instant rise yeast
- ½ cup fine sugar
- 1 ½ cups warm milk
- 2 ½ teaspoons milk (for the glaze)
- 4 ¼ cups flour
- 2 teaspoons cinnamon
- 2 teaspoons all spice

- ½ teaspoon salt
- 1 ½ cups currants
- Zest from 1 orange
- 3 ½ tablespoons unsalted butter
- 1 egg
- ½ cup powdered sugar (for the glaze)
- Caramel sauce or butterscotch (to drizzle on the top)

Instructions:

1. Mix flour, yeast, sugar, all spice, cinnamon and salt in a stand mixer with a dough hook.
2. Melt butter.
3. Add butter, milk, egg, orange zest, and currants.
4. Mix until dough is smooth and elastic.
5. Knead by hand about 10 minutes (yes, you can use your dough hook in your mixer if you want).
6. Place dough in a bowl and cover to rise until double in size.
7. Remove dough and place on a floured surface.
8. Roll into a log shape and cut until you have between 10 and 14 equal sized pieces.
9. Roll into balls and place into a baking pan.
10. Cover and let rise about 30 to 45 minutes.
11. Mix powdered sugar and milk together.
12. Pipe powdered sugar and milk mixture onto buns in the cross shape, using a piping bag or plastic bag with the corner cut off.
13. Preheat oven to 350 degrees and bake for 20 to 25 minutes until top is golden brown.
14. Drizzle caramel sauce or butterscotch over the top for an extra treat.

sticky buns

I adore sticky buns with all the yummy caramel and pecan topping oozing from the top. I wanted something to break up the hot cross buns when I was writing this (not everyone likes them and Sugar Bliss needed to have more pastries), so I thought of sticky buns and mentioned them frequently. You can use the same dough for cinnamon rolls and drizzle them with a powdered sugar icing (see below) instead of the caramel and pecan topping. When I did this (see my TikTok) I made a dual batch of sticky buns and cinnamon rolls to take to an author event.

Ingredients:

- 1 cup warm whole milk (for dough)
- 1 package active dry yeast (for dough)
- ½ cup sugar (for dough)
- 6 tablespoon unsalted butter (for dough)
- ½ cup unsalted butter (for topping)
- 4 tablespoon unsalted butter (for inside)
- 3 egg (1 whole egg, 2 yolks)

STICKY BUNS

- 1 teaspoon salt (for dough)
- 1 teaspoon vanilla (for dough)
- 4 cups flour (for dough)
- ¾ cup brown sugar (for topping)
- ½ cup brown sugar (for inside)
- ¼ cup honey (for topping)
- ½ teaspoon salt (for topping)
- 1 ½ cups chopped pecans (for topping)
- 2 teaspoon cinnamon (for inside)

Instructions:

1. Warm the milk, then mix in half the sugar and the yeast. Cover and set aside until foaming.
2. Melt butter.
3. Whisk egg, yolks, vanilla, and remaining sugar.
4. Add the milk/yeast mixture and butter mixture to a stand mixer and whisk together.
5. Add half the flour and mix until combined.
6. Add egg mixture.
7. Add the remaining flour and mix, using a dough hook until a dough is formed.
8. Transfer dough to a floured surface and knead until smooth and elastic.
9. Place dough in a bowl, cover, and place in a warm place to rise until double in size.
10. Make the topping by combining brown sugar, honey, butter, and salt in a small pot.
11. Place over low heat and stir until butter and sugar have melted.
12. Lightly spray or butter a 9x13 pan and pour mixture in.
13. Top with pecans and set aside.

STICKY BUNS

14. Once dough is risen, preheat oven to 375 degrees.
15. Transfer dough onto a floured surface and roll to flatten the dough.
16. Whisk brown sugar and cinnamon together.
17. Brush dough with melted butter.
18. Sprinkle the cinnamon sugar mixture evenly over the top.
19. Gently roll the long edge of the dough into a tight roll.
20. Cut into 12-13 even sized pieces.
21. Place into your prepared baking dish over the pecan mixture.
22. Bake for about 35 minutes or until golden. Cover with foil after 15 minutes.
23. Invert (turn them over) to serve.

cinnamon rolls

Use the same dough and cinnamon sugar interior as the recipe above, but don't include the cinnamon and pecan topping. Instead, frost with this glaze once they come out of the oven. I will admit, my family liked the cinnamon rolls better than the sticky buns (though they're wrong!).

Ingredients:

- 2 cups powdered sugar
- 2 tbsp butter, melted
- 2 tsp vanilla
- 4 tbsp milk

Instructions:

1. Mix together and spread over the cinnamon rolls.

apple coffee cake

This recipe is what Hattie makes to entice customers back to Sugar Bliss and my editor demanded to get the recipe when she was proofing this book. It was a fun and yummy recipe to make, and my family very much enjoyed it. However, if you watch the TikTok (and know how to bake), you'll see I made a bunch of mistakes. Sabrina and I have a lot in common when it comes to baking.

Ingredients:

- 2 ½ cups flour
- 1 ½ cup flour (for the topping)
- 1 teaspoon cinnamon
- 1 teaspoon cinnamon (for the topping)
- 1 teaspoon salt
- 1 teaspoon baking powder
- 1 cup unsalted butter
- 12 teaspoons unsalted melted butter (for the topping)
- ¾ cup brown sugar

APPLE COFFEE CAKE

- ¾ cup brown sugar (for the topping)
- ¾ cup sugar
- 2 eggs
- 1 teaspoon vanilla
- 1 cup sour cream
- 2 medium apples (Granny Smith or Honeycrisp are perfect), peeled, cored, and chopped.
- Powdered sugar (for the topping)

Instructions:

1. Preheat oven to 350 degrees.
2. In a medium bowl, whisk together flour, cinnamon, salt, baking powder, and baking soda.
3. Beat butter and sugars in a stand mixer with the paddle attachment until creamy.
4. Add eggs, one at a time, beating well after each addition.
5. Add vanilla and mix to combine.
6. Add dry ingredients and mix to combine
7. Add sour cream and mix until just combined.
8. Fold in apples.
9. Transfer batter to sprayed 9x13 baking dish.
10. Combine melted butter, flour, sugar, cinnamon, and a pinch of salt in a bowl to create the topping (it'll look like crumbles).
11. Sprinkle over top of the batter.
12. Bake 50 to 60 minutes until golden and a toothpick inserted in the middle of the cake comes out clean.
13. Let cool completely.
14. Top with powdered sugar.

onion jam

Having Sabrina be a meat lover forced into pretending to be a vegetarian was my husband's idea and one that was fun to play with. I wanted the burger she enjoys at Boundaries to be a craft burger, hence the onion jam. I also wanted something easy I could do a quick TikTok on one evening after my day job. It turned out pretty good, though made the house smell like onions.

Ingredients:

- 4 onions diced (yellow is the best, though red or white are fine too)
- 2 teaspoons salt
- 1 teaspoon olive oil
- ¼ teaspoon clove
- 2 tablespoons thyme leaves
- 1/4 cup apple cider vinegar
- 1/3 cup balsamic vinegar
- 3/4 cup, plus 2 tablespoons granulated sugar
- Zest from 1 lemon

ONION JAM

- Juice from 1 lemon (use the same lemon)

Instructions:

1. Place the diced onions in a bowl.
2. Add salt and mix.
3. Cover and set aside for 60 minutes.
4. Add olive oil to a warmed pan.
5. Add the onions, including any liquid that formed, and cook until translucent, stirring occasionally.
6. Add the clove and thyme leaves, stirring to combine.
7. Add the vinegars and reduce the temperature.
8. Cook for about 10 minutes, stirring occasionally.
9. Raise the temperature and add sugar, lemon juice and zest, stirring to combine.
10. Cook for about 15 minutes stirring occasionally.
11. Remove the pan from the heat.
12. When cool, use immediately.

focaccia

I have a confession; I've never made focaccia in my life or know anyone that has. But it was surprisingly fun and versatile to make. I put olives and tomatoes on mine, but you can put anything on the top to create different flavors. Herbs like rosemary are a popular choice. Chapter 7 is probably my favorite chapter in this book, partially because of the food, including the focaccia I wrote into it. Not sure if mine is as good as what Johnathan and Sabrina enjoyed, but it was still fun to make.

Ingredients:

- 4 cups flour
- 1 teaspoon salt
- 2 cups warm water
- 2 teaspoons instant yeast
- 1 teaspoon sugar
- ½ to 3/4 cup olive oil (you'll use in 1-3 tablespoon increments)
- 2 tablespoons sea salt

FOCACCIA

Instructions:

1. Combine the yeast and water until the yeast foams.
2. Add flour and salt to your stand mixture and mix together with your dough hook.
3. Add the yeast mixture and 1 tablespoon of the olive oil.
4. Mix until dough is sticky.
5. Drizzle 2 tablespoons of olive oil onto the dough.
6. Cover and allow to rise until doubled in size.
7. Drizzle 2 more tablespoons of olive oil onto the dough.
8. Cover and allow to rise again.
9. Add 2 more tablespoons of olive oil to a cast iron skillet and place dough into the pan.
10. Using your fingers, press into the dough, forming dimples and spread it all around.
11. Drizzle remainder of olive oil and add your toppings.
12. Cover and let rise for about 30 minutes.
13. Preheat oven to 400 degrees.
14. Sprinkle sea salt over the top.
15. Bake 30 to 40 minutes or until golden brown.

meatballs

Here's another recipe from the infamous Chapter 7 when Jonathan ordered meatballs and spaghetti and Sabrina couldn't enjoy them. Meatballs are one of those recipes you can't get wrong, so feel free to play with it. I baked them to make them slightly healthier and a bit easier to make. I enjoyed making this one and it doubled as a dinner recipe for my family one night.

Ingredients:

- ½ cup breadcrumbs or Panko
- ½ cup parmesan cheese
- ½ teaspoon garlic powder
- ½ teaspoon onion powder
- ¼ teaspoon parsley
- ¼ teaspoon thyme
- ½ teaspoon salt
- ½ teaspoon pepper
- ½ teaspoon oregano
- 2 eggs
- ¼ cup milk

MEATBALLS

- 2 pounds ground beef (or any ground meat will do)

Instructions:

1. Mix breadcrumbs, cheese, seasonings, and milk together.
2. Wisk eggs in a separate bowl, then add to breadcrumb mixture and mix together.
3. Add the ground beef and stir until everything is combined.
4. Form the mixture into balls (about 1 inch).
5. Heat oven to 425 degrees and place meatballs on a lined cooking sheet.
6. Bake 20-25 minutes until cooked through.

author's note:

Another book done; I can't believe it. Lying, Baking, and Surfing was a pivot for me, but I really enjoyed writing some comedy and getting to know Sabrina and Jonathan. Many of the places mentioned are real, including the Belly Up and Moonlight Beach. Belly Up is a wonderful venue and I highly recommend checking out a show there if you're ever in San Diego. Planes do actually fly between the buildings in downtown San Diego. Stone Brewing and fish tacos are truly an institution along with surfing. I've been lucky enough to have day jobs in Oceanside and Encinitas and you know the waves are good, when you see wet suits hanging from cars in parking lots. Boundaries, the speakeasy mentioned in his book is actually in Temecula and called the Apparition Room—it doesn't have a movie theatre close to it, which is why I relocated it.

Sugar Bliss is completely made up, which disappointed my editor and beta readers who were ready to jump in their car for some apple coffee cake. If you enjoyed these characters, I am expecting them to make appearances in two more books, including one set at that large comic book convention that comes to San Diego every year.

AUTHOR'S NOTE:

If you're interested to know what I listened to while writing this one, it was Goose, Stick Figure, and The California Honeydrops, with some Dave Mathews Band and Brandi Carlile thrown in for good measure.

As always, I have my family to thank; they put up with so much from me so I can spend time on this dream. My soon to be daughter-in-law now comes and asks what projects I'm working on, while playing with the cat. My husband gets a special shout out for listening to my ramblings as I figure out initial plots. He really helped me with this one, increasing how frequently Sabrina got caught in her lies.

I have met such wonderful friends on this journey and in particular, M.S. Ewing and Morrigan, my fellow Semi-Sages of the Pages. I don't know what I'd do without the two of you and your wonderful writing advice, all the laughter, and the support during the bad days. I also have Sarah Faxon, Chris Bannor, Ashleigh Ochoa, and Stephanie Reali to thank as well.

Made in the USA
Middletown, DE
21 February 2024